A Twist In The Tale

FUTURE AUTHORS

EDITED BY ANDREW PORTER

First published in Great Britain in 2023 by:

Young Writers
Remus House
Coltsfoot Drive
Peterborough
PE2 9BF
Telephone: 01733 890066
Website: www.youngwriters.co.uk

Printed and bound in the UK by BookPrintingUK
Website: www.bookprintinguk.com
YB0539U

Foreword

Welcome, Reader!

For our latest competition A Twist in the Tale, we challenged primary school students to write a story in just 100 words that will surprise the reader. They could add a twist to an existing tale, show us a new perspective or simply write an original story.

The authors in this anthology have given us some creative new perspectives on tales we thought we knew, and written stories that are sure to surprise! The result is a thrilling and absorbing collection of stories written in a variety of styles, and it's a testament to the creativity of these young authors. Be prepared for shock endings, unusual characters and amazing creativity!

Here at Young Writers it's our aim to inspire the next generation and instill in them a love of creative writing, and what better way than to see their work in print? The imagination and skill within these pages are proof that we might just be achieving that aim! Congratulations to each of these fantastic authors.

Contents

Ashfield Junior School, Workington

Amelia Hodgson (10)	1
Bella Bailiff (10)	2
Dee Mattinson (10)	3
Grace Fillingham (10)	4
Isabella Hill (11)	5
Lucy Nawrockyj (10)	6
Minnie Hallard (11)	7

Bickley Park School, Bickley

Reuben Thenabadu (9)	8
Melkam Zewde (9)	9
Hari Hogan (10)	10
Kai Taylor-Soong (9)	11
Jake Elder	12

Crazies Hill CE Primary School, Wargrave

Peter Sly (8)	13
Jasper Reynolds-Kasprzyk (7)	14
Ottilie Leatham (8)	15
Sonny Cook (8)	16
George Wetherell (8)	17
Emily Ramsey (7)	18
Zac Miyamoto (8)	19
Sienna (7)	20
Otto Mun-Gavin (9)	21
Bertie White (7)	22
Leo Parsons (8)	23
Claudia Morane-Griffiths (8)	24
Milo (8)	25
Sophia Egarr (8)	26
Alma Berenardini (7)	27
Thomas Elford (8)	28

Cromer Junior School, Cromer

James Petersen (8)	29
Alexander Stewart (8)	30
Malakai Peatling (9)	31
Evelyn Wood (9)	32
Isla Wilson (9)	33
Grace Madeley (9)	34
Ruby Dorras (8)	35

Grainthorpe Junior School, Grainthorpe

Paul Walters (7)	36
Poppy Humberstone (8)	37
Amelia Lenthall (9)	38
Riley Perry (8)	39

Middleton Park School, Bridge Of Don

Isla Kinsey (10)	40
Devin Gilray (10)	41
Callum Wilson (11)	42
Naomi Thomson (10)	43
Quinn Monaghan (11)	44
Laura Egleton (10)	45
Jones Webster (10)	46
Jorgie Cooper (10)	47
Will Uche (10)	48
Naksh Nadagouda (10)	49
James Todd (11)	50
Katie Johnston (11)	51
Nina Innes (9)	52
Mia Gogolinska (10)	53
Harriet Anderson (10)	54
Katie Purvis (10)	55
Kirsty Bea Paterson (10)	56
Benjamin Kirk (10)	57

David Okoro (11)	58
Thea Leighton (11)	59
Aidan Innes (11)	60
Arisha Mahmud (10)	61
Harry Sutherland (11)	62
Raihannat Abd-Rahmane (10)	63
Fraser Gordon (10)	64
Sean Martin (11)	65
Sophia Mearns (11)	66
Xander Cruickshank (11)	67
Grace Philip (10)	68
Ethan James Lynch (11)	69
Dean Mason (10)	70
Sofia Li (11)	71
Calvin Campbell (10)	72
Madeleine Devall (11)	73
Daniel Cooper (11)	74
Emily Bradford (10)	75
Jennifer Anne Killingback (11)	76
Rosie Johnston (11)	77

Ongar Place Primary School, Addlestone

Skyla-Rae Desousa (9)	78
James Lyon (9)	79
Barney Staunton (9)	80
Bella Fenton (8)	81
Robert Rojas-Romero (9)	82
Evangeline Patel (9)	83
Ben Tellling (8)	84
Ethan Davies (9)	85
Louie Rouse (9)	86
Molly Pole (8)	87
Iris Genco (8)	88
Owen Gent (9)	89

Park Hill Junior School, Croydon

Nikki Palav (7)	90
Avni Nagaraja (10)	91
Elijah Guthrie-Alie (7)	92
Akshaj Akshaj (9)	93
Mishika Mehta (7)	94
Ranveer Nanda (7)	95
Christian Molina-Greene (10)	96

Aditi Dhariwal (7)	97
Ishan Yenpure (8)	98
Ihsan Riza Karapoola (9)	99
Adelina Petrachi (8)	100
Rushil Amitkumar (8)	101
Eren Ozer (9)	102

Rose Hill School, Tunbridge Wells

Emily Kench (9)	103
Jess Fenn (9)	104
Louisa Moffat (9)	105
Ella Hiscoke (8)	106
Max Mariner (9)	107
Georgia Dellar (10)	108
Saania Moosvi (11)	109
Romilly Hakes (9)	110
Hayley Rothenberg (10)	111
Vassilys Nitsios (10)	112
Isabella Mattioli (9)	113
Isabella Donnelly (10)	114
Marcus Downs (9)	115
Eliza Craddock (10)	116
Toby Maclean (10)	117
Lydia Coker (10)	118
Ben Hiscoke (11)	119
Emmy Cole (10)	120
Mia Williams (9)	121
Lilly Ferguson (9)	122
Harper Wellings (10)	123
Olivia Springer (10)	124
Mark Scinteie (9)	125
Eliska Krojzl (9)	126
Matilda Whitney (11)	127
Joel Warriner (8)	128
Millie Poynter (9)	129
Thomas Plunkett (11)	130
Aveline Rush (9)	131
Sam Garcia-Hynes	132
Oscar Newton (9)	133
Hugo James (11)	134
Harry Rowton (11)	135
Zara Smith (10)	136
Catherine McKinnell (11)	137
Sam Poynter (11)	138
Sophia Trehan (11)	139

Farrah Walsby (10) 140
Ninuife Mosaku (10) 141
Tobias Harris (11) 142
Joshua Curtis (9) 143
Hari Bhatia (10) 144
Sophia Johnson (9) 145
Harriet Black (10) 146
Isla Bysouth (11) 147
Philippa Smith (8) 148
George Warmington (10) 149
Max Green (9) 150
Louie Rommer (9) 151
Jude Collier (10) 152
Martha Stringer (10) 153
Joseph Johnson (11) 154
Charlotte Currie (10) 155
Ameer Tetley-Ahmad (9) 156
Alfie Loveday (10) 157
Aoife Brennan-Davey (11) 158
Maya Navarro (11) 159
Willow Cureton (10) 160
Henry Whitney (9) 161
Alfred Churcher (9) 162
Caelan Cravero (10) 163
Victoria Hajian (9) 164
Thomas Smart (10) 165
Camilla Wade (9) 166
Joseph Clayton (9) 167
Max Bailey (10) 168

St Helen's Primary School, Swansea

Sunho Kim (10) 169
Mohi Khan (11) 170
Tobias Baldwin (10) 171
Mohammath Faris (11) 172
Ayesha Rahman (11) 173
Sarai Cox (10) 174
Alannah-Jo Owen (10) 175
Dawud Hussain (10) 176

Tushingham-With-Grindley CE Primary School, Tushingham

Roman Jenkins (10) 177
Harry Buxton (10) 178
Georgia Paul (11) 179
Holly Probin (11) 180
Emmy Shaw (11) 181
Freddie Parton (10) 182
Caoimhe Cronin (10) 183
Lola Beckett (10) 184
Frances Hearn (9) 185
Elsie Wilkinson (9) 186
Erica Clark (9) 187
Mckenzie Walker (11) 188
Alfie Dratwinski (10) 189
Harvey Williamson (9) 190
Josh Wilkinson (10) 191
Dayton Meredith (10) 192

The Stories

THE CINDERELLA CALAMITY

"Oh, how I wish I could go to the ball!" Cinderella cried.

Then, as if by magic, a woman appeared.

"Your wish shall be granted," spoke the woman, "but first, you need a dress!"

Suddenly, Cinderella's rags became a beautiful gown.

"Your carriage awaits!"

Without hesitation, she hopped in and set off to the ball. Cinderella had a fabulous night of dancing with the Prince before the stepsisters pounced on her and threw her shoes into the forest! The next day, the Prince came to the sisters' house but knew they weren't his true love. They lived sadly ever after.

Amelia Hodgson (10)
Ashfield Junior School, Workington

SNOW WHITE WITH A TWIST

Snow White, a poisonous ending. Nobody could've guessed this ending would've been executed by one apple, the story starts here. Snow White had gotten kicked out of her lovely house, she found several dwarfs who welcomed her joyfully. One day, what seemed to be an old, ragged woman wearing a cape and carrying a bag full of apples appeared. Unluckily, Snow White answered this old lady; the woman offered her an apple. It was an offer nobody could decline. She took the apple and ate it. It was poisoned. Snow White fell to the floor. Nobody came to her rescue.

Bella Bailiff (10)
Ashfield Junior School, Workington

JACK AND THE BEANSTALK: A TWISTED TALE

It was 6am and Jack had been climbing for one hour, last night he had cried himself to sleep. Turns out magic beans were not a fair swap for his best friend, the cow. Fast forward to 9am, Jack had been climbing through thick cloud for twenty minutes, when his head finally popped up. Nothing had prepared him for what he saw next. Sitting there was God playing the Game of Life with Whitney Houston!

"Excuse me, I was kind of expecting a *giant*," said Jack.

God replied, "You've climbed too far, this is floor two, mate."

Dee Mattinson (10)
Ashfield Junior School, Workington

REFLECTION

As I approached the intimidating building, I felt apprehensive. I opened the door to my new school slowly and walked nervously to my first class where I worked silently. Using all my courage, I tried talking to students only to be ignored. I persevered but still, no reply. Even teachers ignored me! Tears filled my eyes, making everything blurry. I sprinted to the bathroom, wishing I could leave this dreadful school. Whilst washing my tear-stained face, I jumped at the horrifying sight in the mirror. Where was my reflection? Was I a ghost? How had I not realised?

Grace Fillingham (10)
Ashfield Junior School, Workington

ANCIENT SORCERER

Brianna and Brenda lived in a cottage next to the dreary forest, legend had it the forest was home to an ancient sorcerer. They wanted to find the house of the ancient sorcerer. So that night, they packed a bag of sweets and headed off into the blackness of the forest. They peered back at the sweet trail they left. They eventually found it, but it was not what they thought; it was an inside-outside house. As they broke in through the kitchen window, horror filled their eyes. The sorcerer was lying half dead with a knife in his chest!

Isabella Hill (11)
Ashfield Junior School, Workington

THE FOREST

One day, a little girl named Jayden went into a scary and gloomy forest - she was petrified. She saw a huge tree with a secret door. Jayden opened it and went through but it looked the same as the forest she was in before but it was all twisted. She was very puzzled. She started to walk through the forest and she saw a tall, dark figure standing behind a tree. She crept over and there was an unusual man. Suddenly, the dark figure started chasing after Jayden. Quickly, she suddenly lost the man and got home safely.

Lucy Nawrockyj (10)
Ashfield Junior School, Workington

SNOW WHITE

It was late. She had been woken by the terrible thoughts buzzing in her mind. A spitting bundle of rage grew in her head. An idea came to her. She grinned at the thought. She crept out of bed and tiptoed to her damaged sideboard. On it was a sharp object, sharp enough to slice human skin. The Queen's door creaked open, a woman stood in the doorway. Her skin was white as snow, her hair as dark as the night sky and her lips like a red rose. She lifted the sharp object... Death had claimed another victim!

Minnie Hallard (11)
Ashfield Junior School, Workington

I SKIPPED MY ENGLISH LESSON!

Hello! I'm Gordon. Today, something very mysterious happened. My chair started flying in the English lesson! It started when I entered the classroom and sat on my chair. I didn't realise a terrifying experience was coming up... I quickly noticed that my chair was moving. I was flying! My chair lifted me up and zoomed me up and out of the classroom!

"Wait!" cried Mrs Stamp.

I could tell she was very worried and upset because I had a free pass out of English! I was too excited to notice I was going out the window! Wow, what an adventure!

Reuben Thenabadu (9)
Bickley Park School, Bickley

MY LIFE SUCKS

Hello, my name's Jack Zeldi and I'm going to take you through the most terrifying scenes you or anyone may ever witness. It all started when a gigantic boulder came flying into my bedroom. Oh, I'm a prince and my bedroom's as big as a house. Anyway, back to the story. Luckily, I wasn't in there. I was having a stroll in the palace garden. When I saw the rubble, I thought, *today I'll sleep in my second bedroom*. Then I remembered my second room was getting an extension. I'll have to settle for the smaller bedroom; my life sucks!

Melkam Zewde (9)
Bickley Park School, Bickley

BANG!

Bang! My friend fell next to me, it was the middle of the fierce battle between us and the Spanish. Men fell around me, I raised my bow and fitted a poison arrow, aiming at a Spaniard. I let go, it smashed through their left arm, embedding itself in the flesh. Turning away, knowing he was as good as dead, I ran into a hut. Two Spaniards stood in the hut, I stabbed both. Looking out at the devastation, I knew I had to do something. Then a shrill call pierced through the night.
It yelled, "Dinner time, it's lasagne!"

Hari Hogan (10)
Bickley Park School, Bickley

THE FOOD FIGHT

Once, in a magical land in the north, lay the Chicken Nugget Empire. The ruler was Chicken Nugget the VIIth. His son, Chicken Nuggie the Young, loved exploring, but on the east side of the magical land lay the Burger Kingdom. The leader of the burgers was the one and only Cheeseburger the VIIIth and they were sworn enemies with the chicken nuggets. On Friesday, the nuggets and burgers fought whilst Nuggie found a sad, angry pizza who was trying to sabotage the nuggets and burgers. Nuggie fought the pizza and then the foods lived in harmony.

Kai Taylor-Soong (9)
Bickley Park School, Bickley

THE ZOMBIE APOCALYPSE!

Once, there was a boy at school. One day, he was sitting in English when a high-pitched scream was heard, followed by a loud moan, and into the classroom came a green ghoul! It came forwards and bit someone, who shivered and their skin became green! *It was a zombie apocalypse!* Someone screamed as hordes of zombies came into the classroom. People sprinted to hide under the desks, kicking at zombies that got close. The zombies, one by one, turned all of my classmates into zombies, so I jumped out of a window and landed in a bush.

Jake Elder
Bickley Park School, Bickley

MINECRAFT

I spawned in a plain's biome, a great place to spawn. I went to find a tree to punch down. A few seconds later... *bam!*

"How in the world did this tree punch me?"

"I'm alive, can't you see?"

"Okay, but I'm off to find a cave now."

One year later...

"Okay, I am ready to go to the Nether."

Five minutes later...

"I made a portal, time to get in. I'm in, now time to find a fortress."

Two hours later...

"I'm ready to fight the Enderdragon!"

One year later...

"I've done it, victory's mine!"

Peter Sly (8)
Crazies Hill CE Primary School, Wargrave

THE LOST BUS

Everything was going well until a boy called Fin said, "There is a theme park, let's go!"
"No," said a girl.
"Oh," said Fin, "where are we going?"
But then a monster turned the sign.
"Yes, we're going!"
But then the bus crashed. All of the children then saw an abandoned hospital. They went in it. The monster started to chase them. They slammed the door on it. They had to jump out the window. The monster couldn't fit and the children lived happily ever after.

Jasper Reynolds-Kasprzyk (7)
Crazies Hill CE Primary School, Wargrave

AMERICA TO AFRICA

Once, on an American safari, four animals, a lion, zebra, giraffe and rhino dreamed of going to Africa. They fell asleep and woke on the Titanic, they were close to Africa. They were excited, jumped off and landed in the water. They swam to shore and went to investigate a noise. It was koalas singing in a submarine. When they went over, the koalas attacked them. The lion said to attack them back. When he roared, they ran into the submarine. The koalas got out four flower hats and started to sing again so they started to sing as well.

Ottilie Leatham (8)
Crazies Hill CE Primary School, Wargrave

BREAD

Once, a piece of bread was sitting in a swamp of butter and then he found a pig. The pig was running from the cooks and the bread helped the pig stop them. The bread let the pig go but the pig stayed with him. So they went on an adventure, an adventure across the world. The first stop was a dragon's lair. The dragon had a dinosaur bodyguard so they snuck past the guard. There were bear traps everywhere and finally they reached the dragon, it was exhausting. A couple of minutes later the cooks came and ate them.

Sonny Cook (8)
Crazies Hill CE Primary School, Wargrave

THE KINGDOM OF WAKANADAR

There was a boy who was born with the powers of a leopard, they called him Tommy Gun, but there was something wrong with him. he was evil. He was also in the Kingdom of Fire, which was the most powerful kingdom, but Tommy Gun was the most powerful person in all of the kingdoms. If he wanted to, he could take over the whole world. One day, he came to Wakanadar and fought and won. Everyone was scared, but the only thing Tommy Gun wanted was war. The reason why Tommy Gun fought was so he had more power.

George Wetherell (8)
Crazies Hill CE Primary School, Wargrave

THE RABBIT WHO DOESN'T LIKE RHYMING

Early one day, a rabbit was in her burrow with the other rabbits. They loved her because she was famous, her fashion was the best. One day, she came home with a *big* surprise! Everyone hugged her but she had enough. So that night, she went and met a worm, mole and centipede. She tried to talk to them. They couldn't talk so she was sad, but she didn't give up. She was tired and hungry so she dug up into the air and met a sheep. She loved to rhyme until now. She stopped and had a life!

Emily Ramsey (7)
Crazies Hill CE Primary School, Wargrave

MINIONS: THE RISE OF DRU

One day Dru was walking down the wet street. He was walking with his minions Kevin, Stuart and Bob. Dru was secretly a secret agent. He was going to get some ice cream but he saw a shine. He went over. He touched it and he fell into another dimension. Dru found a dead magpie. Seconds later, a giant Cerberus jumped out of nowhere. Dru looked up but he didn't see the sky. He was scared that there was no way out. Suddenly, the Cerberus pounced on him. The Cerberus pulled out a tin of dog food.

Zac Miyamoto (8)
Crazies Hill CE Primary School, Wargrave

THE ENMGAGKAL

Melody was going to get her gift today, she was very excited and her family was too. She walked up the stairs and opened the door and animals ran up to her and asked, "Can we live here?"
She said, "Yes!"
All of the animals ran in and picked her up and ran away, up into the treehouse, and said they wanted to jump and jump. As she got older, her brother's door faded away. Everybody gasped and ran out, and ever since, he has lived in the nursery.

Sienna (7)
Crazies Hill CE Primary School, Wargrave

A CURSED MINECRAFT

A boy called Steve tried to gather some wood, then he teleported to the overworld. He was looking for food in the forest, then he found some pigs being attacked by wolves. He gathered the pork chops and teleported to a coastal village and smelted the pork chop into cooked pork chops. While travelling back, he ran into a woodland mansion that was abandoned. He saw a ghost lurking on the top floor's far corner. When he walked inside, the doors slammed shut behind him...

Otto Mun-Gavin (9)
Crazies Hill CE Primary School, Wargrave

MAGIC

Once, there was a creature. He was called Caney, plus he met a smaller bug. After that, Caney saw a flying train coming to land. Then he met a robot, clean and electrical. Also, he showed Shine the robot magic dust. But sadly, Shine shut down. Plus he took the magic dust. Soon after that, the train took Shine in the flying train. But Caney jumped onto the train. Caney grabbed Shine and jumped off the train, also resetting whilst falling, and they lived happily ever after.

Bertie White (7)
Crazies Hill CE Primary School, Wargrave

BRIGHTSTORM: THE FRIENDLY WOLVES

Once, there was a little ship that crashed in a forest. The Brightstorms started to wander around. Then they found Dad's ship. It was amazing! They got in Dad's ship and they found the puddings. When they got off the ship, they got back to the ship and slept. After that, they got found by animals called the Thought Wolves. As they approached the Thought Wolves...

"Argh!" said Ben.

But the Thought Wolves said, "Can we be friends?"

Leo Parsons (8)

Crazies Hill CE Primary School, Wargrave

THE TIGER, THE WITCH AND THE FLOWER POT

Clara, Ranter, Edwood and Hazel were evacuated from their home because of the war. One day, they were playing hide-and-seek. Clara fell into a flower pot and landed in a magical land called Lartia. The others fell in too but Edwood got cursed by the Black Witch. Luckily, Clara heroically saved him by throwing a sharp piece of ice at the wicked witch and they all became kings and queens of Lartia. The top tiger was really proud but Clara never forgot her sword.

Claudia Morane-Griffiths (8)

Crazies Hill CE Primary School, Wargrave

CAT MAN SAVES THE WORLD

Cat Man is running from the major and finds a trap. Then he cuts the wire and makes a boom! And then the mayor gets boomed. The mayor gets sent to the hospital with a broken leg and spends two days in the hospital and it is very painful. Suddenly, Cat Man gets sent to the hospital to become a human again. Now he can drive he is not as cheeky. Then he gets stronger, now he can lift a car and a boat and he goes to the gym four hours a day.

Milo (8)

Crazies Hill CE Primary School, Wargrave

THE FLOATING BLUE

Far, far away in a magical land lay a forest. Next door sat a small cottage. The cottage belonged to Hansel, Gretel and their wicked parents. One day, the children were sent out to collect berries when they saw a blue light. They followed it and it led them to a witch! At first, they were quite scared, but they did grow to like her. The witch turned Hansel and Gretel into a wizard and witch and they lived happily ever after.

Sophia Egarr (8)
Crazies Hill CE Primary School, Wargrave

RAPUNZEL

One day, a pair had a baby girl, and then she saw a vegetable and stole it from the witch. The witch found out and stole her. She took her to the forest. One day, a prince was riding a horse and heard her sing. The prince rode to the palace to find a pair of scissors but it was in the tallest tower. He brought her the scissors and cut off her hair and made a ladder out of her hair and escaped and lived in the castle.

Alma Berenardini (7)
Crazies Hill CE Primary School, Wargrave

STAR WARS: THE EVIL DRAGON

Lukus Mikewalker was living on the planet Patowene. His sister, Lily, was trapped in the Death Star because Darthing Man knew that she had stolen the way the Death Star worked. Lukus and the old man, Obi Woning Kobi, went and saw Han Poslo and his friend Chatterbaccer. Then a dragon came to Patowene and nearly destroyed everything in sight. *Boom!*

Thomas Elford (8)
Crazies Hill CE Primary School, Wargrave

RED RIDING HOOD WITH A TWIST!

One rainy day, Little Red Riding Hood was angrily stomping to her grandma's house. Little Red Riding Hood didn't like her grandma's house.

When she was in the middle of the woods, she met a wolf and she said to the wolf, "I have to go to my boring grandma's house."

The wolf just went silent and walked into the trees. Little Red Riding Hood just walked to her grandma's house.

When she arrived, Grandma said, "Come here, little child."

Little Red Riding Hood didn't come, instead, she gobbled her and the wolf. She thought, *take that, Grandma! Haha!*

James Petersen (8)
Cromer Junior School, Cromer

THE DRAGON ESSENCE

Atop a snowy mountain, a cave was punctured on the side. Inside, a massive dragon was preserved perfectly in ice. Suddenly, it shattered into a million pieces. The dragon was free, and with one wingbeat, it was off into the sky.

"Finally, I got out of that frozen dump!" said the ice dragon as he flew down to the village for a human snack. "*Ow!* What was that?"

A flaming arrow had just hit his side and he turned into a human! He plummeted from the sky.

A dragon-killing sorcerer called Hugo Antonoid said, "*Muahaha!* I killed a dragon!"

Alexander Stewart (8)
Cromer Junior School, Cromer

LITTLE GREY WOLF

Deep in the cave lay a little grey wolf, he was going to Wolfmother's.

His mother said, "Don't talk to humans."

He said, "Yeah, yeah, bye Mum."

He set off, following the road. He came across a wolf hunter.

The man said, "Where are you going?"

The wolf said, "I'm going to see Wolfmother."

The man rushed to Wolfmother's house and put on a great old nightgown and got into Wolfmother's bed! The wolf came up to the cave. The wolf went inside. He saw the man, ran and hid...

Malakai Peatling (9)
Cromer Junior School, Cromer

THE DRAGON

This is the story of the one dragon.

Once, there were some children. They all thought they would get a new place to hang out, but when they arrived, there was an unexpected turn... You see, they came to a cave where the dragon lived but he awoke when their laughs and screams awakened him as his raging raging anger grew again. They smelled the danger coming from the smoke from his flames.

The dragon whispered, "Soon."

The children came back again and again. Every year, the dragon came closer and closer to the afterlife, day by day.

Evelyn Wood (9)
Cromer Junior School, Cromer

SOPHIE'S MYSTERIOUS CHRISTMAS

One snowy winter, Sophie was so excited about Christmas. She was counting the days. At Christmas, all of Sophie's family went to Granny's house. Some of her family left but Sophie and her family stayed. Everyone was playing games and it started to snow. It was finally Christmas Eve and they were having fun. But they all stopped and went to bed. The next morning, they all woke up and went downstairs to find one present each. They didn't really care because they all knew that Christmas was only about spending time with family.

Isla Wilson (9)
Cromer Junior School, Cromer

THE GOOD ELF

There once was an elf that was helping Santa so the presents got to where they needed to be. Santa always said to the elf, "You're doing a good job now."

The next day, the elf was found in the workshop, making the presents but there was an elf who was bad and came to the elf and gave him a sweet to eat. The elf took the sweet and ate it and he turned into a bad elf too, so then Santa was not impressed with him. From then on, who knew what he did...

Grace Madeley (9)

Cromer Junior School, Cromer

RED PANDY

Suddenly, a twig snapped behind a green bush so Evie wondered what it could be. So she quickly shoved all the leaves to the side and found a really cute panda that was a small cub, curled up on a twig with a nice green leaf attached to it. Evie picked it up and carried it in her arm and hands, warm from the bonfire, and she sat the panda on a nice log until it growled. So she went to go and fetch some bamboo for it to eat, but suddenly the panda was gone...

Ruby Dorras (8)
Cromer Junior School, Cromer

THE PRINCESS IN DISGUISE

Once, long ago, King Duncan rode out, hunting for deer in the gloomy forest. Without warning, Goliath reared in terror, throwing Duncan onto the muddy, wet ground and galloped away. In the twilight, Duncan shuddered as he felt breathing behind him. Before he could move, a ferocious beast leapt upon him. The huge, gargantuan wolf kept biting the king more and more. Bleeding profusely, taking his last breaths, Duncan stabbed at his attacker. It groaned in pain. He peeled the disguise to reveal it was actually Princess Martha! As tears rolled down her sorrowful father's cheeks, Princess Martha laughed maniacally.

Paul Walters (7)

Grainthorpe Junior School, Grainthorpe

THE CAT'S PICNIC

Once upon a time, there were seventeen magnificent cats going on a picnic. If you go down to the park today you'll be sure of a massive surprise. If you go down to the park today you'll be sure of a big picnic. You can play games like cats' tig and hide-and-seek. It's time for your mummy cats and daddy cats to pick you up because tired little cats go to bed and get tucked away and think of more fun picnics. Your dog friends are coming tomorrow. Have a good night's sleep and have some good dreams tonight.

Poppy Humberstone (8)
Grainthorpe Junior School, Grainthorpe

CRIMINAL IN DISGUISE

Once, there was a girl named Shantel Spice. You might think she was a perfect lass but she wasn't. She was as clever as a canary and as fast as a ferret. She was a criminal, she stole from many families but it was for a reason, she was so poor. The first family she stole from was the McTurners. In total, she stole £400 so they went looking for her. She got richer every minute. I was walking for hours until I finally found her, that monster. I finally caught her and took her to jail, behind bars.

Amelia Lenthall (9)
Grainthorpe Junior School, Grainthorpe

MY PET SHEEP IS EVIL

I live in the dark, deep woods with my pet sheep, he is so fluffy. One day, we went on a walk to a water fountain in the park that had monkey bars that sheep could play on as well as any animal in the world. The sheep turned against me and started to demolish the park and everywhere and in my house and it was heartbreaking to me and my heart. I started to cry, everywhere was demolished, everywhere! The house was demolished and so was everything in his path!

Riley Perry (8)
Grainthorpe Junior School, Grainthorpe

TIMEWORKS

Imagine a world that always rains and suddenly goes to clear skies. Well, that's what happens here in Warped Woods. It always rains, but one day Ellie was walking in the rain, but as soon as she checked the time on her pocket watch it went sunny and time stopped... but she could still move.

"I can still move?" said Ellie, "But that's impossible?" she murmured.

So she called her best friend. The call was answered.

"Victoria!" Ellie said. No reply. "Victoria?" No reply. *"Victoria!"* she shouted.

"Haha, got you!" said Victoria.

"You're okay!" said Ellie.

"Yes..." Victoria said.

Isla Kinsey (10)
Middleton Park School, Bridge Of Don

LIFE OF NESSIE

Once, at Loch Ness, lived the Nessie family. The kind twins went fishing and never came back again. They looked and looked.

"I give up," said Tim.

"Hurry up," said Kelp.

"Let's keep searching," said Tom.

"*Argh!*"

Two dead bodies were on the floor and covered in an ink-like substance on the shore. It was the twins! Who did it?

"I think Tom did," said Tim.

"No, I'm not the killer!" said Tom.

"You are!"

"You're accusing me for nothing!"

A knife flew at Tim and he died!

"Argh!" screamed Tom.

Kelp smiled, it was him the whole time!

Devin Gilray (10)
Middleton Park School, Bridge Of Don

THE MUM WHO WAS A MCFLURRY

One frosty evening, a boy called Michael was so hungry so he said, "*Mum*, I'm hungry!"
She answered, "Yes, dear?"
"I'm hungry!"
"Okay," she answered, "let's go to McDonald's."
"*Yay!*" he said.
So they got into the car and drove to McDonald's. When they got to McDonald's, they ordered some food. When they got their food they went to a table to eat.
After they finished eating, Michael's mum started acting weird so he asked "Mum, are you okay?" But before she could answer, she turned into a *giant* McFlurry and Michael screamed in terror!

Callum Wilson (11)
Middleton Park School, Bridge Of Don

FRIENDS FOREVER

Matilda and Karen were the best of friends, they did absolutely everything together. They were an extremely mischievous pair, which got them into lots of trouble. Especially the time they covered their strict teacher in shaving foam. On Monday, they decided to play a prank, but it went wrong. Instead of covering their pushover supply teacher in custard, they covered their headteacher in custard! They were shut in Karen's garage. Karen decided to play with her dad's sharp axe.

Matilda said, "Stop swinging that around, you'll hit someone."

Karen retorted, "I don't care!" swiping the axe at Matilda, killing her.

Naomi Thomson (10)
Middleton Park School, Bridge Of Don

ORDINARY FLOWER

Multiple twigs snapped underneath the gardener's feet as he got closer. The sun was shining brightly upon the precious flower, who was standing still as any ordinary flower would. Shrieking loudly, the lawnmower came closer.

Across the big garden was a little girl called Lily. *Oh no!* she thought to herself. She was frozen for a moment, but then she sprinted as fast as physically possible.

"Stop!" she screamed.

The gardener was extremely startled.

"That flower is really a girl called Freya. She and I can both transform into different things!"

"I am utterly shocked!" he said, looking frightened.

Quinn Monaghan (11)
Middleton Park School, Bridge Of Don

AWESOME ART

There was a beautiful, smart, and creative young woman called Symphony and her black cat Francisca. They lived in an art studio in France. She had many perfect paintings but her favourite painting was of the underworld... Strange, right? One day, the ground began to shake vigorously! She and Francisca fell into the painting of the underworld... When she opened her eyes, they were being carried by monsters and the monsters were shouting, "*Sacrifice, sacrifice...*"
Suddenly, the painting started to crack and all the monsters fell... Symphony grabbed the edge but Francisca betrayed her! Symphony fell into the endless abyss!

Laura Egleton (10)
Middleton Park School, Bridge Of Don

MISTAKE AT MYSTICAL MONKEY COVE

Greg and Robert were fighting. Greg hit Robert with his huge legs. The battle was unimaginable. Greg, wub overlord, was the victor. Robert shook his fist with rage, seeking revenge. Greg teleported to the ancient wub temple and Robert flew to his house. *Crack...* There was an intense rolling noise... *Kaboom!*

"Argh! Help!"

Robert tried to fly but he couldn't so he ran. He finally got there. The scream was from none other than Greg, wub overlord. Robert picked up the boulder.

"Hahaha!" he laughed in a villainous voice and squashed Greg.

Robert was evil all along!

Jones Webster (10)

Middleton Park School, Bridge Of Don

CHRISTMAS' TRIP TO THE NORTH POLE

Hello, I'm fantastic Phoebe. On the 1st of December, my elf, Candycane, brought me a hamster called Christmas who had luscious brown spots all over her smooth fur. Nobody could touch Candycane, but one snowy, winter's night, Christmas touched Candycane, taking all her magic. That night, Christmas flew to Lapland and found a key to get into Santa's wonderful workshop. Christmas entered the workshop but got caught by all the elves and ended up at a girl called Holly's house. Coincidently, Holly was Phoebe's BFF! When Candycane found out, she got Christmas back, replacing her with another hamster called Snowpop.

Jorgie Cooper (10)
Middleton Park School, Bridge Of Don

AMONGESE.....

In a sussy spacecraft bought by Elon Musk, Bebe Yoda went to the fridge to get some noodles. It was hilarious, like when Mr Toilet roasted Discord Mods. Suddenly, a wild impasta yeeted out the fridge, dancing like a mindless alien dog. Meanwhile, Discord Bots were chasing Mr Toilet, as swift as... a snail?

"Your face looks like a dog's bone!" he yelled.

Amogus exited the Discord-themed game and yeeted her normal computer into the Tree of Dababy!

Grandpa zoomed in like, "What's going on?"

Chicken broke in. Sus boy fled to... Ohio? Chad Guy Clown was dating Amogus Ladies.

Will Uche (10)
Middleton Park School, Bridge Of Don

THE LAVA BRIDGE

Harry and Joe were best friends in primary school, academy, and university, and they always trusted each other. One day, they wanted to cross the Lava Bridge, so the next day they crossed the Lava Bridge. At first, they were scared, but they were going to cross anyway, and it was as hot as lying in fire. Harry was burning intensely, but Joe said it was fine so they crossed. While they were halfway across the bridge, Joe pushed Harry into the lava.

Harry screamed, *"Help me!"*

Joe shouted, *"Hahaha!"*

Harry shouted, "I never should have trusted you!"

Naksh Nadagouda (10)
Middleton Park School, Bridge Of Don

THE PREDICTION

Luke is dreaming, it's one of his 'special' dreams because Luke can predict the future.
As Luke arises from his slumber, his mum shouts, "Get ready, the psychologist will be here soon!"
As Luke eats his breakfast, the psychologist walks through the door.
"Hello, you must be Luke."
"I am," Luke says glumly.
As they are talking, Luke tells him about the dream.
"I saw your death, I was standing there, looking at you as you fell to your knees, screaming." Luke takes the knife he is hiding and swings it. "This is your fate."

James Todd (11)
Middleton Park School, Bridge Of Don

ROAD TRIP TO OHIO

It was an average day in Ohio. The Toddles family were packing up to go on a road trip so they got everything ready and headed off to the middle of nowhere in Ohio.

The mother was nervous about what she was about to say but she said, "I'm actually the son of this family..."

"And I'm the family dog..." replied the grandma.

"And I'm the family daughter..." said the dad.

"*What the actual heck?*"

Timothy unbuckled his seatbelt and smashed the window with his foot and rolled out of the car, never to be seen again. Bye, Timothy...

Katie Johnston (11)
Middleton Park School, Bridge Of Don

A VISIT TO GRANDMA'S

Little Red Riding Hood, or Little Red, was visiting her grandma when she bumped into a wolf. The wolf asked her where she was going - wait, you know the story. Or do you? She finally got there and knocked on the door but no answer, strange right?

"I'm coming in!" Little Red said fiercely.

She walked in but her grandma wasn't there. She saw a wolf! She ran outside where the woodcutter was. Pulling the axe out of the woodcutter's hand, she went inside.

"*Stop!*" said Grandma, she hit Little Red!

The wolf and Grandma lived happily ever after.

Nina Innes (9)

Middleton Park School, Bridge Of Don

LITTLE RED RIDING HOOD

Once upon a time, there was a girl called Little Red Riding Hood. She went to her grandma's house. She thought it was the sweet, wonderful grandma but it wasn't her...

She asked Grandma, "Why do you have such big, dark ears?" She asked scaredly, "Why do you have such big, yellow teeth?"

The wolf said, *"To eat you better! Muahaha!"*

Then Little Red Riding Hood ran out of the haunted, creepy, smelly, soggy cottage and the soggy, creepy woodcutter was outside and cut Little Red Riding Hood up instead of the big, bad, scary wolf!

Mia Gogolinska (10)

Middleton Park School, Bridge Of Don

YoungWriters
Est. 1991

THE MYSTERY RIOT!

Once upon a time, on a dark and gloomy night in winter, Sara was walking home from school. All of a sudden, her phone pinged. Her friend Daniel texted her.

'Where are you?'

'I'm on my way home.'

'Do you know about the riot?'

Sara was confused. Apparently, two criminals had escaped prison and were following random people. Sara was about a mile away from home when a man dressed in black appeared. Sara was put into a van a minute later and taken away. Daniel answered the door of his home and the criminals were there with something unexpected...

Harriet Anderson (10)

Middleton Park School, Bridge Of Don

FOXCRAFT

They'd made it to Elder Rock, Siffrin had told Zarka that the Elders were her one hope to find her brother and for Haiki to find his family. The Elders talked in one voice.

"You seek your families and brother, Simmi and Tao."

The two foxes jumped at their names.

"Your family is alive, Haiki, your family is alive and Zarka your brother is alive." There was a pause.

"It's just too bad you won't be seeing them."

And just like that, Siffrin and the Elders attacked them. They tried to fight back but there was no hope for them!

Katie Purvis (10)
Middleton Park School, Bridge Of Don

WOLFIE: THERE ARE TWO SIDES TO EVERY STORY

Everyone knows the three little pigs. Wolfie tried to eat the poor little pigs. I just don't think it's fair the pigs got to tell their side; there are two sides to every story. It was a cold, damp night when the pigs called Wolfie and invited him around for tea. He accepted and set off through the woods. When he came across three houses, he wasn't sure which pig was hosting so he went to each. Finally, he arrived at the brick house.
"Thanks for having me, my fridge was empty."
"Same, that's why you're here!" said the pig.

Kirsty Bea Paterson (10)
Middleton Park School, Bridge Of Don

GAME TIME: THE FINALE

The 70s, where it all began. Cube World had a diamond that made Cube World. If it was destroyed, Cube World would die. Scramble Stewart tried that once but failed because of our superhero, Cuber Campbell. Scramble Stewart was in Cubism Asylum for the Evil. He had a plan to destroy Cube World but he wanted to get rid of Campbell first. By trapping him in a ginormous game gallery. So he escaped. That night, Campbell was guarding the ginormous game gallery. Scramble Stewart came running at Cuber Campbell but Campbell suplexed Stewart and he fell in the never-ending gallery...

Benjamin Kirk (10)
Middleton Park School, Bridge Of Don

BOB'S EERIE DREAM

Bob was relishing his day, from winning a lottery to being crowned the king of the minion world. Frolicking like he was in a world of his own, he gnawed on his vanilla-flavoured chocolate and decided to go outside for some fresh air. He noticed the earth was grumbling; assuming it was an earthquake, Bob did not move. Eventually, Bob perceived smoke, identified a grey sky, and observed buildings collapsing.

"Oh! It is the end of the world!" wailed Bob.

All of a sudden, a witch emerged. Bob shrieked in horror. Then he discovered it was just a dream.

David Okoro (11)
Middleton Park School, Bridge Of Don

SPY DAD

This story starts on one normal day in New York City. Izzy had just woken up and was going downstairs for breakfast, she had bacon, eggs and toast.

"Hey, Izzy," said Mum.

"Hey, Mum. Oh, by the way, have you seen Dad?" asked Izzy.

"No, he said he was going on a work trip," replied Mum.

But little did they know he was out working for the government and had been spying on them for months and just hadn't said anything. Later that month, they found out and kicked him out of their family, but he wasn't done spying...

Thea Leighton (11)
Middleton Park School, Bridge Of Don

PEELY THE BANANA

One morning, Peely looked out the window and saw a car pull up. It was a new neighbour whose name was John. Peely heard lots of noises and it was John.

Peely said, "Keep it down."

"*No!*"

"Fine," said Peely.

Peely went back to the house and took his hamster out. Peely turned into Dusty. Dusty, now human, put Peely back in the cage. Dusty went to the World Cup Final, it was Argentina versus France. Then the neighbour sat next to him and then they had a fight! Suddenly, Peely woke up and it was all a dream.

Aidan Innes (11)

Middleton Park School, Bridge Of Don

CREEPY PASTA OR NOT?

Once, in a land of food called Sheep Land, there were talking foods. But one in particular really stood out and her name was Penne Pasta, but the thing about her was that nobody wanted to be her friend. So one day, Penne had enough of nobody wanting to be her friend. Then she went to a wizard, his name was Nick Nacho, so Penne told him everything.

He said, "Oh, don't worry, everyone will want to be your friend after you drink this."

"Okay," she said shakily and drank the potion.

But instead of everyone liking her...

Arisha Mahmud (10)

Middleton Park School, Bridge Of Don

THE MAN ON THE MOON

George looked out his big blue telescope and saw what looked like a tall, dark figure smiling menacingly down towards him.

"What's that?" George asked himself.

He ran inside and asked around his house to no avail. Confused, George sprinted back outside and gazed back out his telescope, although this time the man was faint and almost ghost-like. George walked around the telescope and wiped the lens with his finger. George was intrigued to see if the man was still there... But he wasn't! It was a smudge on the lens after all!

Harry Sutherland (11)
Middleton Park School, Bridge Of Don

THE TERRIFYING DREAM

Once upon a time, there was a girl named Kirsty and she was very kind. One morning, she woke up and found out that she had a new neighbour, Isla. She went over and they immediately became friends. They did everything together but got into a lot of weird trouble, but Kirsty didn't know that Isla was actually a spy sent to kill Kirsty and she was desperately trying to get Kirsty into trouble. If not, she would be killed instead, and finally, Kirsty was killed. Suddenly, everything went tremendously dark and Kirsty woke up. It was all a dream...

Raihannat Abd-Rahmane (10)
Middleton Park School, Bridge Of Don

THE KILLER CAT!

Once upon a time, Dwayne Johnson AKA The Rock bought the White House. Three months later, he bought a cat. Donald Trump did tell him that the cat would make a mess.

He said, "Oh well. He is a good cat, not a bad cat."
Donald Trump said, "Okay, don't get mad at me if he ruins it."

The next morning, the house was destroyed. Dwayne was trying to hide it but he had a meeting with Donald Trump. Minutes later, Donald arrived. He was looking for Dwayne but could not find him. He was horribly scratched to death.

Fraser Gordon (10)
Middleton Park School, Bridge Of Don

BLUE CAP ELF...

Jim is known for working hard in Santa's Workshop, being nice and having a bright blue cap. Christmas is here! So he climbs into Santa's sack, but falls out into a random house! The next year, Jim shows himself. A boy called Joe finds Jim in the morning and is delighted. But during the night, Jim does horrid things. Until one day, Jim sets a fire, but he keeps moving! Joe's dad sees Jim in action. Shocked, he calls the fire brigade and police. But when they get there, he's already left. All that is left is a blue cap...

Sean Martin (11)
Middleton Park School, Bridge Of Don

LOST AND FOUND

Once upon a scary, dark night about two years ago, there was a girl called Veronica. One morning, she woke up and was in a forest. She thought she must have been kidnapped. Two more hours passed and she was stuck. Her parents were so worried, they tried calling her but it went straight to voicemail.

Meanwhile, at her house, her parents called the police but nobody could find her. One night, she felt strange and thought she was being carried. Surely enough, she woke up in her house and went to find her parents but they were gone...

Sophia Mearns (11)

Middleton Park School, Bridge Of Don

FINLAY THE FOX

It was Finlay's time to shine, he and his dad sprinted towards the farmyard, but they had to be cautious because there was a big guard dog. Suddenly, the big dog dived onto Finlay, but his dad jumped in to save him.

Finlay said, "Oh no! What's that stomping?"

They turned around and there was the farmer with a big shotgun. Finlay knew what he had to do, he made a fake dart towards the woods but stopped. *Bang!* The farmer had missed and both foxes immediately flew at him and turned to dust.

Xander Cruickshank (11)
Middleton Park School, Bridge Of Don

THE MAGIC CROCODILE

Once, there was a farmer called Jim who owned a crocodile called Crocs. Crocs was outside and he was looking around and found a rocket, he accidentally stood on it and he shot up to space. He landed on the moon. He was floating and met some aliens who touched Crocs. Crocs went sparkly but then the aliens pushed Crocs down to Earth. Crocs woke the next morning on Mount Everest. He blinked and then he was in Hawaii. He blinked again and he was in Edinburgh. He closed his eyes and Jim woke up, it was all a dream...

Grace Philip (10)
Middleton Park School, Bridge Of Don

TWIST AND A TALE

One day, there was a boy named Joe. He was a very nice boy, living with his grandpa and his mum. One day, he went walking at 9 but something was wrong. It didn't seem right, there was no one outside but himself. He didn't care, then he saw someone.

The man came over and said, "Come with me," and he did.

Then he transported him to the jungle.

Then Joe asked, "What's your name?"

He said, "Mystery Man."

Then the man disappeared so he sat down...

Ethan James Lynch (11)
Middleton Park School, Bridge Of Don

THE SCARY NEIGHBOURHOOD

Once upon a time, a new neighbour moved in. I went to the local store and bought a welcome card for the new neighbour. I went to the house and knocked on the door. The new neighbour looked nice, and kind at first. I went back home, after giving him the card and getting to know him. I went to sleep.

Suddenly, I woke to a window being smashed. Someone then shot a bullet into the house.

I called the police and the FBI. The FBI broke down the door and shot the guy.

The guy was my new neighbour.

Dean Mason (10)
Middleton Park School, Bridge Of Don

THE UNIVERSE OF CHRISTMAS

It was no ordinary Christmas Day. My mum and dad gave me a beautiful snow globe as a present. It was magical. When you tapped it three times, it would take you into another world! But I didn't know that when they gave it to me. I was in my bed, playing with the snow globe. Then I tapped it three times to make the fake snow fall. Suddenly, I was sucked into the globe, screaming as I went. "Argh!"

Then, I landed with a thud. I looked around me. There was snow everywhere. Where was I...?

Sofia Li (11)
Middleton Park School, Bridge Of Don

A TWIST IN THE TALE

One morning, Kai gets an unexpected letter from his dad who he has never seen. He wants Kai to come and see him but Kai's mum doesn't approve. She thinks Kai's dad is dangerous but Kai wants to go but his mum won't let him. Suddenly, a portal opens. It sucks him in. It takes him to a snow desert, and then suddenly a mummy sees him. The mummy feels like he knows Kai and asks if he can go home and have Christmas dinner with him. They are all very happy and they all become a family again.

Calvin Campbell (10)
Middleton Park School, Bridge Of Don

BEANS VERSUS SPAGHETTI HOOPS

Once upon a time, the Bean Team were chilling in Beanalto's cosiest tomato spring and all of a sudden, the Spaghetti Cools strutted in, looking all smug! The Spaghetti Cools vandalised their favourite tomato spring by tipping three tons of dry ice into it. Luckily, the beans took action! The beans took bean acid guns and squirted them all over them! The Bean Team was about to win, but to my surprise, Sonic wandered in, looking for a snack! Sonic spotted the tasty beans and took a large scoop...

Madeleine Devall (11)
Middleton Park School, Bridge Of Don

THE GIANT AND THE MISUNDERSTANDING OF A PYRAMID

One bright, sunny morning, a giant called Somasama the Great woke up in his cold, muddy cave and walked outside and saw a gigantic pyramid in front of his cold cave. Somasama wondered if the pyramid would be warmer than his freezing cave. Somasama strolled towards the pyramid but he stopped and his eyes stayed fixed on the heart of the pyramid. It grew arms and legs and started walking towards Somasama, picked him up and threw him to the Thames all the way from Egypt. The rest is a mystery...

Daniel Cooper (11)
Middleton Park School, Bridge Of Don

CINDERELLA'S NOT-SO-HAPPY EVER AFTER

Cinderella came into the ball, looking as gorgeous as a queen. The prince came over and asked if she would like to dance. She said she would love to! But then suddenly the clock hit midnight and she ran away before anything was said.

The prince took the slipper and came to Cinderella's house and tried the slipper on her. It fit but he thought she was too ugly so he tried it on the ugly sister. It didn't fit but he thought she was gorgeous so they lived happily ever after.

Emily Bradford (10)
Middleton Park School, Bridge Of Don

A WALK IN THE WOODS

It was a frosty, snowy day and I went out into the woods. I fell into a deep hole and goblins suddenly kidnapped me. I was freaked out. The goblins froze me and then left me for a while. Soon later, the goblins kept looking at me and they looked hungry. They licked their lips, then...
I woke up and heard my mum's voice saying, "Wake up, it's time for school!"
I was so happy it was a dream.

Jennifer Anne Killingback (11)
Middleton Park School, Bridge Of Don

THE MAN IN THE WINDOW

It was a late night, Sapphire was lying in bed, doing nothing when she heard something smash in her neighbour's house and a scream, so she decided to go investigate. She opened the door to her neighbour's house and got snatched! Suddenly, she could see again and it was her grandma. Yes, it was her grandma, and she had murdered them! "You're a murderer, Grandma!"

Rosie Johnston (11)
Middleton Park School, Bridge Of Don

DANCING BEAUTY

Ding! Dong! They'd arrived. The door opened aggressively as guests came barging in. Music was booming in the background. The guests were raving and rocking to the beat while the disco ball lights glimmered. Dancing Beauty's parents rolled in their beds, disturbed by the faint illumination. The room was shaking like an earthquake, the party poppers were excited. Suddenly, the disco ball was clinging to the ceiling for dear life. It didn't manage to survive the hectic party below, descending to the ground. Then Dancing Beauty's parents suddenly came marching down the stairs, they couldn't believe their exhausted eyes...

Skyla-Rae Desousa (9)
Ongar Place Primary School, Addlestone

THE MIDNIGHT MAN

"Argh!"

A girl called Lily was running away from something that had recently given her a deep cut. Her thoughts had recently been turning into reality, but this thing was a person. A man. A midnight man, or Lily's husband (whatever you prefer). The cut began to sear painfully. Lily was too busy worrying about the pain that she tripped over a stump and fell. Her vision went blank. She awoke, she wasn't in the woods, though. Her lamp was blinding her eyes until an unrecognisable shadow loomed over her.

She called, "Is someone there?"

It was her handsome husband...

James Lyon (9)
Ongar Place Primary School, Addlestone

BROOKHAVEN CRIMES FAIL

One ordinary night in Brookhaven, Dude1867BS was strolling down the road, yelling for a taxi to Main Street. A taxi arrived and he hopped in. When the taxi arrived, he jumped out. However, as he was a police officer, anything could pop up. Dude1867BS got in but his phone rang, it was his neighbour. He said the bank had been robbed so he rushed straight over. As he arrived, nothing had happened.

The phone rang again, the neighbour said "Don't forget, it is number 23 Crown Point."

He wailed the siren. He pulled up but saw not what he expected...

Barney Staunton (9)
Ongar Place Primary School, Addlestone

LITTLE YELLOW HOOD

There was once a little girl called Little Yellow Hood, because she was always sunny side up. She wanted to go see her great-grandad to give him some lovely bright flowers. She set off the next morning with them. She happily walked until she met a fox. She was very scared, so ran off to hide until he was gone. The fox took a quicker route to Great-Grandad's house. When he got there, he took the great-grandad's clothes and put them on. He pretended to be Great-Grandad. Yellow Hood arrived and could not work out why Great-Grandad looked so different...

Bella Fenton (8)
Ongar Place Primary School, Addlestone

THE SUSPICIOUS BEAM

Every night there would be a beam but it wasn't an ordinary beam. It wouldn't be visible during the day, only at night. There was a theory that it was a signal of some kind. People said that in the beam there was a container and in there were robots going along Area 51, discovering secrets, special weapons and more. They said the president was in danger, but suddenly a military base encountered the beam and immediately set off to search. They knew where to go, they just didn't know the exact location. Finally, they got there and stopped it.

Robert Rojas-Romero (9)

Ongar Place Primary School, Addlestone

THE LITTLE BLUE PRINCE'S HEAD

Princess Bella said to her mum, "I'm going to a party."

So off she went on her horse. Bella knocked on the door. The door swung open. Bella charged in. They were dancing, they were enveloped with excitement and then they were very hungry. They had food like crisps, sweets, pizza, yoghurts, chocolate, fudge, and sandwiches. They watched a story time and a colossal spider came out of the TV and scared them all. They screamed out loud. The parents came to them and got a pan and then hit the spider. Bella went back home sad.

Evangeline Patel (9)

Ongar Place Primary School, Addlestone

RONALD AND THE FOOTBALL

War! War! It was time for the match. Ronald got his red uniform and slipped out onto the illuminated green field, full to the brim with footballs everywhere, and the match began. There was a red football with a cheesy grin. The football didn't like Ronald because last time he had a trip to Mars. So he slapped Ronald when he took the penalty. Ronald got put on the bench till halftime. In the other half of the match, he got ten goals because the red football liked Ben and Ben was on Ronald's team, but the football still succeeded...

Ben Tellling (8)
Ongar Place Primary School, Addlestone

THE WITCH WHO MADE HISTORY

Once, in 1777, there was a witch who made history. But years before, she was just a girl with no mum and dad. One day, she was finding a place to sleep. However, she spotted a book, a mysterious book. It was a spell book. You could command spells like levitation. But ten years later, in 1777, the witches now competed against the wizards. The wizards had most of the land. The witches fought against them. They made their comeback. It was the end of the wizards' reign. The witch who did the most was the heroic Scarlet...

Ethan Davies (9)
Ongar Place Primary School, Addlestone

LITTLE GREEN RIDING HOOD

Little Green Riding Hood's favourite colour was green. She even loved vegetable parts that were green. Her bed had a green pillow and cover. But every Sunday, she would visit her grandma and bring her some food. So this Sunday, she went there, however, she wasn't there when she opened the door. Meanwhile, her mum was at home, chilling on the couch, watching TV, when she rushed to put her shoes on. As she left the house and ran to the woods, she rushed towards the scream from Little Green Riding Hood...

Louie Rouse (9)
Ongar Place Primary School, Addlestone

FIRE RED

There was a girl who was in the woods. She was walking. She heard a noise on one side then the other, then someone popped up behind her! They had green eyes and red hair. Then the person behind her cast a spell on her. Her hair was on fire now. Her name was Fire Red. Two years later, she was the worst villain ever. Once, she put a bomb in a building and it exploded everywhere, but everyone got out of the building before the bomb exploded. Luckily, nobody was in the building. It was so terrifying and scary.

Molly Pole (8)
Ongar Place Primary School, Addlestone

THE EARTHQUAKE

Once, a little girl was at school. She was in her first class, literacy. She was learning about Iron Man. She really liked Iron Man. There was a really big shake. Everyone in the classroom ran and went into a shelter. It stopped, and an aftershock came. She had a roller coaster of emotions. It was a really bad day because it was raining as well, but the only good thing was her dad's birthday, so she was very happy about later at least. That was the only good thing about today. She walked home...

Iris Genco (8)
Ongar Place Primary School, Addlestone

LITTLE WILD WOLF BOY

Little Wild Wolf Boy was never calm, was always wild and wore a wolf costume. There was only one thing he was afraid of and it was Little Red Naughty Hood. She was annoying because she kept pranking him and scaring him. For instance, he was walking to his grandma's house and she pretended a wolf had eaten his grandma. When he found out, he jumped on top of Little Red Naughty Hood. She never pranked him again. As for Little Wild Wolf Boy, well, he got a punishment and did not do it again.

Owen Gent (9)
Ongar Place Primary School, Addlestone

MUNGO'S ADVENTURE

Long ago, a monkey called Mungo wanted to fly to a beach. So, he painted a picture of an aeroplane with his magic paints, which turned his paintings into real life. Mungo flew in the aeroplane to the beach where he crash-landed.

He found some mysterious footprints. He followed them to find Charlotte, who was searching for something in the sand!

As Charlotte turned around and saw Mungo, she exclaimed with joy, "Mungo!" She ran and quickly picked him up. She said, "Mum, I found Mungo!" She then muttered to her favourite *stuffed toy*, "Oh Mungo, where have you been?"

Nikki Palav (7)

Park Hill Junior School, Croydon

BEACH ADVENTURE

The emerald sea glittered like diamonds. An athletic man took in the chalk cliffs and the shimmering sea. Grabbing his surfboard, Jacob bounded off the rocks and splashed head-first into the clear water. As he slowly advanced deeper into the sea, control slipped from his grasp. *Crackle!* The storm began, Jacob's face paled and his curly locks swept into his green eyes. Gusts tugged at him. He fixed his eyes on the massive waves rapidly approaching. He tried to swim away but like two giants locked in combat, the waves collided with each other, sending him soaring into the air...

Avni Nagaraja (10)
Park Hill Junior School, Croydon

BLUE AND CHOCOLATE'S TERRIFYING RIDE

There was an active boy called Chocolate and a cool-looking cat called Blue. One day, Blue told Chocolate, "I am no ordinary cat, I have magic, and I want to take you on a carpet ride."
Blue said, "Miaow, magic, magic carpet ride, turn yourself to magic time!"
Boom! They flew into the air like an aeroplane. They slowly approached a large cave with ancient markings. They saw a dragon, a zombie ghost, and the boss! They were terrified! He was ginormous and tried to steal their souls. Blue used another spell to get home. They promised to tell nobody...

Elijah Guthrie-Alie (7)
Park Hill Junior School, Croydon

THE MYSTERIOUS SHADOW

Sarah awoke from her dream, shivering. Her room was as dark as coal and she could see the shining stars through the windows. Suddenly, she saw a glimpse of a shadow on the blank wall. Jumping out of bed, wondering what to do, she crept through the dark, discoloured and dingy corridors. As she walked further, the shadow grew bigger and scarier with sharp teeth. Looking around her parents' room, she tried to find a torch. Finally, she pulled out a drawer and found one. Scampering quietly downstairs, she scanned the room hurriedly until she got to the dining room...

Akshaj Akshaj (9)
Park Hill Junior School, Croydon

BANANA THAT DOESN'T LIKE ITS NAME

Once, there was a banana that was extremely unhappy with its name. It felt like it was so ordinary and boring. One day, the banana decided to take a walk around the world to find its perfect name. As it travelled, it asked everyone it met for suggestions on what it should be called. The first person it met was a giraffe, who suggested the banana be called 'Tall'. The next person it found was a tiger, who suggested the banana be called 'Fierce'. Finally, he met a monkey who called it 'Yummy' and ate it all. Poor Yummy banana.

Mishika Mehta (7)
Park Hill Junior School, Croydon

THE TITANIC AND THE NOT-SO-REAL STORY!

The Titanic, a luxury ship, was sailing on the icy Atlantic Ocean when a watcher saw an object in the sea. The watcher screamed and the ship swerved left. But something happened. The Titanic went through the iceberg and started zooming inside it. People fell down, but most of them managed to hold on. It was a *portal to another world!* The other world was called Merotopia. People flew off and got lost forever. The people enjoyed their new lives in Merotopia, a beautiful place full of adventures with lots of buildings and good restaurants.

Ranveer Nanda (7)
Park Hill Junior School, Croydon

SCHOOL TRIP GONE WRONG

Hello, I'm here to tell you about my school trip and how it went terribly wrong. So this is how it went. We were on the bus and I saw a big, bad tiger.

I yelled, "Argh! Tiger!"

I told Miss and nobody believed me.

So we stopped and Miss said, "Here we are."

When we got off the bus and they all saw the fierce tiger, they ran back inside and closed the doors.

I said, "*Told you!*" in fear but they did not say anything.

So we went back to school. We all lived happily ever after.

Christian Molina-Greene (10)

Park Hill Junior School, Croydon

ANIMAL JOURNEY

Once, there was a bunny named Elisabeth, a dog named Redy and a Fox named Clara. One day, they found a portal, it was so cool, it looked like a black hole! The three animals went inside the portal and suddenly they flew, sliding all the way to... the Antarctic! It was freezing cold, so chilly! They almost began to freeze! A polar bear saved the three animals. The animals felt blessed for their rescue. They hugged the polar bear. Finally, the portal came near the ocean and they jumped and flew all the way back to their place, Wales.

Aditi Dhariwal (7)
Park Hill Junior School, Croydon

THE UNTOLD STORY OF RAPUNZEL

Once, Rapunzel was walking in a forest, suddenly an old granny captured her and imprisoned her in a clay tower. Then, a peasant came along. Rapunzel straightened an old wig when the granny came. She put the wig away and hurried to the window. The old lady threatened her and went away. After putting the wig on, Rapunzel hurried to the window to impress the peasant. The wig caught his eye, he now wanted to save poor Rapunzel. He had an idea, he climbed on her wig but it fell! The hot wig melted the clay tower, burying the trio.

Ishan Yenpure (8)
Park Hill Junior School, Croydon

ANTIVE THE AGENT

Once, there was a boy named Antive who wanted to go on an adventure around the world. He wanted to explore countries around the world. Until one day he found a machine where if you typed a country name into it, it would make you disappear and you would get into that certain place. So he typed in Sydney, Australia and he was an agent, so he took his stuff and he saw a monster called Thorrathes and when Antive used his powers he hit the core of Thorrathes and defeated him. Antive was called a great and powerful hero!

Ihsan Riza Karapoola (9)
Park Hill Junior School, Croydon

THE TRUE STORY OF THE TITANIC! BY THE CAPTAIN

People say that my ship, the Titanic, got sunk and blah, blah, blah... But let me tell you the real way, people! So, one day, my crew were sailing on the Atlantic Ocean and all at once we saw an island! We sailed towards the island and we slept and ate on it for months until we saw a giant squid come and smash a hole in our ship! The squid squirted ink at us and people died, but a few people managed to get on the lifeboats and survive!

Adelina Petrachi (8)
Park Hill Junior School, Croydon

THE WEIRD FUNCTIONED CAT SAT ON THE MAD DOG'S MAT

One day, a very weird cat sat on a mad dog's mat. But the cat made a big mistake. The dog came down and felt like falling on his *face!* The cat got scared and jumped out the window. The dog chased after the cat. The cat ran and ran into the streets, he got so tired he got slow, and then he got cornered by the dog's friends. The dog took the cat home and warned him never to do that again. They became best friends.

Rushil Amitkumar (8)
Park Hill Junior School, Croydon

THE SKILLED TIGER

Once upon a time, there was a man, his name was Rao. One day, Rao was going to a forest and he found a tiger. The tiger had a lot of cool moves, so Rao made the tiger go hunting so he could make him money. At first, the tiger was happy, but then he realised that the man was using him. The tiger got mad and attacked the man.

"*Roar!*"

Then the tiger was calm. Did you get scared?

Eren Ozer (9)
Park Hill Junior School, Croydon

THE CHASE

"Eley, where are you? Um, excuse me, where's the big, black elephant?"

"Oh, that one, she left a few days ago..."

"But didn't I tell you to reserve her?"

"Sorry, did you use our email?"

"Yes, why?"

"Our email isn't working."

"Oh no! What zoo did she go to?"

"We can't give out information like that."

"Ugh, how am I going to find her?"

"That's your problem. Have a good day."

"Eley, is that you? I've looked everywhere! Um, excuse me. Can I adopt this elephant?"

"Sure, ID please."

"Here."

"Okay, all set! Here's your toy."

"Thank you so much!"

Emily Kench (9)
Rose Hill School, Tunbridge Wells

GOOD TRY

Bang!

"Yes, I did it, I've finally gotten rid of that stupid building!" Guy Fawkes declared from a small rowing boat he'd fled from the scene of the plot in. But suddenly, a tiny, high-pitched voice squeaked, "Hold it, I'm Crimson, head of the FleaBl, and you're under arrest."

"But I can't see you!" Guy exclaimed.

"Look at your lantern," Crimson replied.

When Guy looked, he burst out laughing.

"Go on, little fly, or whatever you are. Arrest me."

At that, Guy shook Crimson off the lantern onto the cold, smelly deck, lifted his foot and stomped down hard. *Splat!*

Jess Fenn (9)

Rose Hill School, Tunbridge Wells

A TOIL WITH TROUBLE

I woke up with a start and looked around at where my family had been. They said they'd be back late, but not this late. Were they walking our dog? No! Suddenly, a girl leapt out of the bushes, screaming, "Help, my family's missing!"

"Your family's missing?"

She said they were kidnapped during the night. We exchanged names.

"Aphrodite," she laughed.

I giggled, "Valerie."

We ran and discovered a cave. Sneaking in there, they were all tied up.

"*Run!*" both families screamed.

Untying them, we sprinted home! The kidnappers were making tea, so we had some tea and made up.

Louisa Moffat (9)
Rose Hill School, Tunbridge Wells

DARK DREADERS

4H were having a science lesson when, without warning, the bones they were identifying came to life! There was a loud crunching sound from the left and everyone turned around to see such an extraordinary creature - half dog, half rat!

The creature squeaked, "Ah, got my parts mixed up."

Everybody was confused.

"What's going on?" asked James Jackson.

Henry Cop said, "I don't know, but I'm out of here!"

The creature mumbled, "We are dark dreaders, our spirits come to life at night. Promise to keep our secret or die."

James answered hurriedly, "We promise to keep your secret!"

Ella Hiscoke (8)
Rose Hill School, Tunbridge Wells

PLANET WARS

Planet Wars. On a star very close by...

"The rebels are going to blow up this base! Everyone, get ready! They are coming any moment now," said Darth Vader.

One hour later...

"Where are they? Send out ships to check it out!"

"*Go, go, go!*" yelled a Stormtrooper.

"Okay, what are we looking for?" asked the Imperial rookie pilot.

"Um, I think I found it! It's the live ball! How are we supposed to blow it up?" Blue Five said.

"Look, a trench! We are going in."

Darth boomed on the intercom, "All X-wings lock S-foils in attack positions..."

Max Mariner (9)
Rose Hill School, Tunbridge Wells

THE SNOWY PROBLEM

The icy Arctic wind howled across the snow. Greta, the ancestor of Roald Admundson, was surveying the polar bears. She looked up at the magnificent Northern Lights and noticed a shooting star; it landed at her feet. Greta asked, "I wonder what you are?"

The star introduced herself, "I'm Twinkle Twinkle the little star."

"What do you do?"

"I twinkle like a diamond."

"Please can you help? The satellite is faulty and I can't get my data back!"

Twinkle twinkled, "No problem, I can send your data by twinkling in Morse code."

With that, she shot up into the sky!

Georgia Dellar (10)
Rose Hill School, Tunbridge Wells

THE ESCAPE GONE WRONG

"Come on, it has to be somewhere," Jennie exclaimed, as she frantically searched for the key. At last, she finally found it. Rose, her friend, also thought she saw something. Jennie looked, and then the worst thing happened. She couldn't find the key!

"What, where did it go?" Jennie cried.

"I have no idea," Rose uttered.

Suddenly, Jennie found the key for a second time and as they clambered towards the door Rose accidentally nudged Jennie, which made her drop the key again. *Could someone be sabotaging me?* Jennie thought. *Could it be Rose? No, Rose wouldn't do that. Right?*

Saania Moosvi (11)
Rose Hill School, Tunbridge Wells

SWEET VICTORY

"She's going to eat us. I know she is!" whimpered Hansel.

"Stop snivelling and let me think," whispered Gretel.

The gingerbread door creaked open and in hobbled the decrepit old hag. When she reached the children's cage, the witch stretched out a bony, green finger.

"Wait!" stammered Gretel. "I admire your willpower to settle for two skinny kids when you could have a juicy, plump adult."

Later that evening, the children sat by the raging fire, eating souvenir sweets from the gingerbread house roof while the witch settled down for a big, steaming bowl of stepmother stew.

Romilly Hakes (9)
Rose Hill School, Tunbridge Wells

THE END OF THE WAR

Splash! A bomb crashed into the ocean. Starletta, the sea dragon, shot into the air, narrowly missing a flying dagger. It was the Dragon Wars. Suddenly, everything went white.

"Stop fighting at once," commanded the stern voice of the mystical Dragon God.

Colour returned to the scene, but all the dragons' weapons had vanished and been replaced with beautiful roses and colourful paper hearts! Magical dragon dust glinted over Starletta and the other dragons in the sunlight, and they immediately began flying or swimming to a member of the other army and exchanging hugs and smiles. The war was over.

Hayley Rothenberg (10)
Rose Hill School, Tunbridge Wells

BATTLE OF THE AGES

"Finally, we've won the war. It's over!" one of the knights declared.

Lord Nine said to himself, "I'll regain my full power," whilst the king patted him on the back. "Come," he exclaimed, "we have to celebrate."

However, Lord Nine didn't want to celebrate. He decided to wait until the king was drunk so he could kill him for his power and kingdom.

"Although the prince, his son, would get the kingdom if the king died," Lord Nine whispered to himself. A guard was close, heard everything and ran to warn the king.

Lord Nine killed him and the king...

Vassilys Nitsios (10)

Rose Hill School, Tunbridge Wells

STORM BLACK

You all know the fairy tale 'Snow White'. Well, did you realise she had a sister? Not an annoying sister - a sincerely kind one. However, everyone disagreed. It started one Christmas. Storm sprayed perfume over all the gifts which eventually got to Snow's apple, ruining her Christmas and making it taste like tulips. When Snow White blamed Storm, she got into an argument with her father. However, her stepmom supported Storm because she was her favourite. Once Snow's kiss happened, everybody forgot about Storm. Seven years later, Storm found her own man who truly loved her. She's still traumatised today.

Isabella Mattioli (9)
Rose Hill School, Tunbridge Wells

THE TALE OF THE MYSTERIOUS FIN

One beautiful afternoon, Ella and Jane were enjoying the stunning sunshine. There wasn't a cloud in the sky and the sea was glistening. Ella and Jane were looking over the horizon and suddenly, Jane noticed a grey object coming close to the boat.

"What's that?" asked Jane.

The object coming closer was obviously a fin!

"It's a shark!" shouted Ella.

They both looked at each other in fear. A shark had attacked not long ago.

As the shark got closer, a woman shouted, "Come on!"

Suddenly a head came up. Phew! It was only a child wearing a plastic fin!

Isabella Donnelly (10)
Rose Hill School, Tunbridge Wells

JUNGLE RUNNERS

"Ah," sighed Fred, "I miss Bobby!"

"Yeah, he was lovely. He was a Westie, wasn't he?" asked Josh, as they all sat around the fire.

"Wait! What was that?" asked Sirius, his voice full of panic.

Everyone was screaming! Max grabbed his bow and arrows.

"It's a horde of monsters," he said, "we need to fight them off."

They all jumped into the heat of battle. Monsters were left and right, but together they managed to defeat all but one. As he swung his huge axe, Max shot his last arrow. It hit it square in the chest, killing it.

Marcus Downs (9)

Rose Hill School, Tunbridge Wells

MY FUNNY DREAM

I went to Rosehill for breakfast club, but they served me lunch, not breakfast. *Okay*, I thought, *I'm late!* So, I rushed to maths with Mr Stacey, but he was teaching English!

"Why are we doing English? It's maths now!" I asked Mrs Wilson.

She just laughed! Next, we had hockey, but everyone took their hockey sticks to the swimming pool.

"How can we play hockey in the pool?" I asked Mrs Wren. "The ball will get wet."

But she just laughed!

"Eliza!" my mum shouted. "Are you up?"

Then I woke up; it was all a dream.

Eliza Craddock (10)
Rose Hill School, Tunbridge Wells

THE BIG BOOM

World War One. 1914. The war was raging, but not all was sad. Parts of the trenches started making truces since it was Christmas. Soon, everywhere was peaceful and England and Germany played a football match. One person, Jeremy, hated football and was running around like an idiot. He spotted a mound and thought, *that's a good mound to jump on!* So he jumped on it. A ginormous explosion started. *Kaboom!* He thought that Germany had placed a landmine, but then confetti sprayed everywhere and German soldiers came out with Christmas presents. Finally, the English came out and exchanged presents!

Toby Maclean (10)
Rose Hill School, Tunbridge Wells

THE NEW GIRL?

Hi, I'm Zoe. There is a new girl starting at my school and I've offered to be her buddy. I'm so excited to meet her. She is starting *today!* My teacher says that she is very good at academic subjects, but will need help with more creative subjects and sports. Her name is Roberta and she should be arriving any minute now. I can't wait. I hope that she is best friend material. Hold on; what's that strange noise? It's getting louder and louder. All I can hear is a *clink, clank, clink, clank, beep, beep.* Could it be Roberta?

Lydia Coker (10)
Rose Hill School, Tunbridge Wells

HARRY POTTER SURVIVES

Harry Potter has come from his Charms class to join his friends in the vast dining hall. Suddenly, Dumbledore arrives and starts trying to put a killing curse on Harry.

He furiously waves his powerful and pointy wand and shouts, "Avada kedavra!"

Hermione and Ron jump up frantically and try to save him, but he's too powerful. Out of nowhere, Lord Voldemort leaps out from a hanging chandelier and protects Harry with a magical invisibility cape. Together, they manage to bring down Dumbledore by turning him into a funny-looking pink house elf and he explodes with a huge bang!

Ben Hiscoke (11)

Rose Hill School, Tunbridge Wells

TWISTED BEAUTY

As the princess lay in her everlasting slumber, the prince gazed over her and said, "I dreaded the day of your sweet sixteenth birthday."
Suddenly, he heard a deep voice.
"Kiss her... Maybe the tales are true."
The stunned prince thought it was only him and the princess in the castle.
The voice demanded again, "Kiss her."
And so, he did. But to his shock, the princess melted away into ink. At once, the prince realised this was neither a fairy tale nor a wonderland, but a nightmare come to life! There wouldn't be a happy ever after, after all!

Emmy Cole (10)
Rose Hill School, Tunbridge Wells

FROM DARK TO LIGHT

Once, there was a dragon called Peril. She went to Evil Dragon School. She was red, orange and dark yellow. Peril's teacher, Mr Mooshie, always made Peril do good things. One day, Peril snuck into the boys' bathrooms and put a slime thrower in Drake's locker. As she shut it, she heard a toilet flush and glared at the boy that emerged. The boy gasped and ran into the showers.

When he emerged, he cried, "Peril, please become my loyal, good dragon!"

Peril gaped and cried, "Oh yes, yes, yes!"

Together, the land was protected forever by the two heroes.

Mia Williams (9)

Rose Hill School, Tunbridge Wells

THE GIRL WHO CRIED STRANGER DANGER

There once was a girl who played pranks. One day, she was bored and thought of a prank: it was to say there was a stranger.

"Mum, there's a stranger!"

Her mum ran as fast as she could, but no one was there.

The next day, the girl said it again, *"Mum, there's a stranger!"*

No one was there.

Her mum said, "Don't jinx it!"

The next day, the girl heard a knock. This time there really was a stranger.

"Mum, there's a stranger!"

Her mum didn't come and the man kidnapped her.

Lilly Ferguson (9)
Rose Hill School, Tunbridge Wells

WINNIE-THE-POOH

In a land far away, there lived a boy named Christopher and a couple of teddies named Winnie, Eeyore, Piglet and Tigger. Winnie was fond of honey. One morning, Winnie found himself stuck up a tree, in search of honey. Hearing shouts for help, Christopher and the others ran to his rescue. Christopher spread out his scarf and said, "Winnie, jump!"

"But what about my honey?" Winnie said, as he hesitated to let go of the tree. Pooh jumped. "Woohoo!"

With a big splash, he had fallen into a huge pot of honey. It wasn't at the top after all!

Harper Wellings (10)
Rose Hill School, Tunbridge Wells

THE MISSING HONEY

One day, Pooh was hungry so he plodded over to the cabinet where, to his surprise, his very last pot of honey had vanished.

"I must track the thief down," he thought aloud.

So, off he went into the woods. In front of him, he saw a trail of sticky honey. Pooh was excited, a clue at last! He trotted quickly down the hill until he came to a clearing and there, eating a honey sandwich, was Christopher Robin!

"*My honey,*" exclaimed Pooh indignantly.

Guiltily, Christopher Robin turned around, just as a blob of honey rolled down his chin.

Olivia Springer (10)
Rose Hill School, Tunbridge Wells

A TWIST IN A TALE

This story is set in 1485 during the Tudor times. It was a bright morning and I was strolling past a tinker and suddenly he started to beg on his knees. He raised his ragged hat and pleaded for money. "Please can I have some money? I'm really poor." And then he started sobbing. Since I'm kind, I was midway reaching in my pocket for some cash when one of the king's guards came up to us and shouted, "Didn't you hear the king? No street beggars, you filthy vagabond!"
And then grabbed the tramp and said, "Come with me!"

Mark Scinteie (9)
Rose Hill School, Tunbridge Wells

HER STRANGE LIFE

There once was a girl called Hetty. She went to a boarding school called Croachusity. The headmistress, Miss Croachsum, was no ordinary headmistress; she was a malicious witch. She threw children into her magical pool. When children got pushed in, it felt like they were being poked with 100 needles. Soon, a lady called Jen took Hetty to her mansion. When she'd unpacked her bags, Jen told her to *never* go into the attic. A few weeks later, Hetty became suspicious of Jen, so one evening she grabbed her torch, pen and paper. Curiously, she stepped into the attic...

Eliska Krojzl (9)
Rose Hill School, Tunbridge Wells

THE MONSTER UNDER MY BED

One evening, I was sitting on my bed, engrossed in my new book. Suddenly, there was a scuttling from beneath my bed! I jumped down and peered apprehensively into the darkness. Deep, green eyes fixed on me. I screamed in horror! My mum rushed in as I was pointing to the bed. She reached underneath and pulled out a fluffy, discarded old teddy. She turned and left, shaking her head. But then I saw something red dripping from its mouth, the dog collar around its neck and a slow wink. "Has anybody seen the dog?" mum shouted anxiously from downstairs.

Matilda Whitney (11)
Rose Hill School, Tunbridge Wells

THE GREAT ESCAPE

I was in the Gladiator Prison where the most dangerous criminals went. I'm prisoner 7045. It was a damp, dark autumn day. Rain trickled down the window as a mouse scuttled along the floor. I was sick of this place. I needed to escape, but how? I rounded up a gang; this was the day we would disappear. Miraculously, we discovered there was a secret passageway behind a picture. We crawled through the soggy tunnel. We heard a crumble; the tunnel collapsed, killing comrades. I was distraught, but I realised there was no turning back, this was the great escape.

Joel Warriner (8)
Rose Hill School, Tunbridge Wells

THREE LITTLE PIGS

Hello, I'm Mr Wolf. You think I'm scary, but I'm innocent. What the three pigs forgot to tell you was I'm a building inspector. My job was to test how strong their houses were. It was an accident! I didn't mean to blow Porky and Ham's house down, but sticks and straw weren't the best material to build a house with. Bacon was much smarter, he chose bricks. Now, let's talk about Bacon's house... He wouldn't let me in, so I had to go down the chimney. Not my brightest idea... I still have the bottom bruises to prove it!

Millie Poynter (9)
Rose Hill School, Tunbridge Wells

THE BIG BANK ROBBERY

There were ten of them, we won't go into names. They were planning on robbing the London bank. Here was the plan, five of them would dig a hole underneath, break into the vault and grab the loot. The others would be on lookout. After a lifetime of digging, they were below the vault. One of them sent a message.

"Go time."

Boom! The bomb was too powerful. The bank blew up. They all heard a ringing noise. They all went silent and stared at each other. They knew what it meant.

"Home time!" the teacher said.

Thomas Plunkett (11)
Rose Hill School, Tunbridge Wells

THE NIGHT OF THE MONSTER...

There once was a shy, twelve-year-old girl called Molly. She lived in a quaint cottage in a sleepy village. One day, she heard her neighbours talking about a scary monster with eight hands that they had seen in a nearby wood. Molly sprinted home, terrified, and dashed inside. She ran upstairs and noticed a mysterious note on her bed which said: 'I am your cousin, meet me in the garden'. Molly ran to her window and saw a sinister shadow outside. She felt as cold as ice, as eight big hands rested on her shoulders. Then, everything went black...

Aveline Rush (9)
Rose Hill School, Tunbridge Wells

DASH FOR FREEDOM

Suddenly, I found myself in the halls of a vast castle; the ceilings reaching to the sky. I only had moments to take in my surroundings, before noticing a demon, which seemed to be following me. I decided to run. I began sprinting down the many corridors of the castle while avoiding other mythical creatures. I needed to be quick, as the hideous demon was still on my heels. I needed a weapon, and fast! I dashed into an immense dungeon, filled with the most petrifying beasts I'd ever seen. Suddenly, the world in front of me began to disintegrate...

Sam Garcia-Hynes
Rose Hill School, Tunbridge Wells

THE MINOTAUR CAME TO SCHOOL

On a bright, sunny morning, we heard the fire bell, as normal. But midway through going outside, we saw and heard strange things. Scared, we began to move faster. The Minotaur was there! Petrified, we screamed and ran. Tripping over my shoelace, I flew forwards and hit my head. I woke up, relieved it was only a dream. Then I realised where I was. Not in my bedroom, house or school. I was somewhere oddly familiar. I recognised it from my history lessons, the Minotaur's maze... The lights turned on and there it was. The Minotaur, ready to eat me!

Oscar Newton (9)

Rose Hill School, Tunbridge Wells

WHAT IF JORDAN WENT ON THE HOGWARTS EXPRESS IN HIS SECOND YEAR?

Once, Jordan and Charlie were on platform 5 3/4, they said goodbye to Mrs Wain. They met Hermy on the train, found their own compartment and sat down. The trolley wizard came past with tempting whacky wizard sweets. Moments later, whilst talking, a person came in and stunned them. Then they awoke. Hermy tried to check her watch but realised that she was Jordan! Jordan was Charlie and Charlie was Hermy. They rushed off the train and told Ruben, who took them to see Wizardo. He changed them back, but nobody could quite work out how it had happened.

Hugo James (11)
Rose Hill School, Tunbridge Wells

A STRANGE MURDER

There had been a murder. The vice president was dead. The detective sent in was called Dan Davis and his partner John had discovered that the murder weapon was a sharp instrument. His partner was a brilliant detective called John Slate. John had solved countless cases with Dan. They were making no progress with their case, and after a long day at work, Dan invited John for a drink at his house. When John arrived, they had a good time talking and drinking until way past midnight. When John went home and fell asleep, that's when Dan struck...

Harry Rowton (11)
Rose Hill School, Tunbridge Wells

THE THEATRE'S SURPRISE

One day, Lulu and her parents went to the theatre. They had just sat down when a large tentacle flopped down onto the stage. Suddenly, the actress gave a blood-curdling scream. The monster sucked her up and blood flew into the audience. Babies were crying and children were screaming, as their parents grabbed them and sprinted to a safer place. As the power went out, Lulu noticed a red glowing light coming from behind a small door. She cautiously walked through the rows of seats to discover the monster snacking on the chairs' foam cushions...

Zara Smith (10)
Rose Hill School, Tunbridge Wells

A SWEET MATHS LESSON

Dot was a normal girl. An overweight girl. Dot loved chocolate. Dot often got teased about her size and her love of all things sweet but she couldn't care less. Dot was used to being bullied and it didn't bother her. One day, when Dot was in maths, she was craving chocolate, it was all she could think about. Then suddenly her fingers started to tingle, a shot of energy blasted through her fingertips and the desk turned to chocolate, solid on the outside with a gooey centre. Everyone stared at her. What on Earth had just happened?

Catherine McKinnell (11)

Rose Hill School, Tunbridge Wells

THE SWITCH

The kids wanted to play a joke on their dads on April Fools. Their dads were Harry Kane and Joe Root. They wished their dads would switch sport jobs for the day. Surprisingly, their wish came true! There was a massive surprise at White Hart Lane when Harry Kane had been dropped and Root was playing! The same shock was felt at Lords. At half-time, both teams were losing horrendously! Kane kept kicking the ball at the stumps and Root kept throwing the ball into the goal. The kids needed to make another wish, but what an April Fools' joke!

Sam Poynter (11)
Rose Hill School, Tunbridge Wells

MYSTERIES IN LESTER

I'm Kira and I'd just moved from California to Lester, where bad things happened. Mysterious actions occurred, and five weeks later this wanted poster appeared of a strange man right on the lamppost in front of our house! Three months later, new people moved in next door to us. I soon became best friends with the girl my age; Tracey. After eight weeks, she invited me over, but when I got there I noticed she was extremely rich! She told me where my coat went, but when we headed down for dinner, her father was someone unexpected...

Sophia Trehan (11)
Rose Hill School, Tunbridge Wells

CHRISTMAS GONE WRONG

The night before Christmas, Santa and his elves were getting ready for the big night, but something wasn't right. Santa checked the reindeer and all were fine.

While they were throwing the massive sack in the back of the sleigh, Mrs Claus made some cookies and Santa gobbled up his favourite ones without delay.

As Santa tried to take off, the reindeer would not fly so Santa started to worry as he thought Christmas was over. Luckily, with a simple bit of magic, Mrs Claus made all of the reindeer fly again. Christmas was still on!

Farrah Walsby (10)
Rose Hill School, Tunbridge Wells

THE TWIN EXPLORERS

In the pool, Scarlet, Ivy, Ariande and Rose had been invited to a lovely hotel in Portugal after saving the world so many times. While they were swimming, Rose saw a mysterious glow from the forest.

Rose exclaimed, "Hey guys, I saw something cool and interesting! Wanna go see it together?"

"*Sure!*" shrieked the girls.

They set off after they had dressed. When they got to the glow, they found a beautiful waterfall cave and the glow got brighter! They went into the cave and explored curiously...

Ninuife Mosaku (10)
Rose Hill School, Tunbridge Wells

HILL VALLEY SCHOOL

I go to Hill Valley school. A new boy joined our school last week. His name is Pepe Mariano, he is from Spain, he speaks perfect English. The boy was shy at first and didn't want to play at break time. We talked him into joining and he did. He was better than all of us combined! We played a football match for our school and Pepe's dad came in a Lamborghini! It turned out his dad is *the* wonderful, magnificent Lionel Messi! Everyone was astonished and we all got his signature on our games kits! What a surprise!

Tobias Harris (11)
Rose Hill School, Tunbridge Wells

THE HIDEOUS MONSTER

A man called Brian worked in a noodle bar. He was serving a customer and noticed something unusual behind the sticky counter: a hideous monster with countless tentacles and a small head was hiding there. The monster jumped onto the innocent customer. Brian tried to grab one of its tentacles but it was slippery and slid out of his now slimy hand. The creature lolloped down the road to create more destruction but Brian expertly got out his lasso and captured it. Everyone cheered but it broke out of its lasso and went on a rampage.

Joshua Curtis (9)
Rose Hill School, Tunbridge Wells

SPINNERMAN

In the Marvel Universe, there is a superhero called Spinnerman whose powers are that he can spin around at 200mph. Spinnerman used to work for Iron Man, so he is naturally good. Spinnerman is very tall. To be exact, he is ten foot two inches. As well as being that tall, he is also as clever as a dolphin and an elephant combined. Spinnerman can also control air like in Avatar. But then Spinnerman gets into a fight with Dr Strange. Spinnerman lands a big wind gust on Dr Strange's legs and kills him. Maybe he is bad after all!

Hari Bhatia (10)
Rose Hill School, Tunbridge Wells

THE GREAT ESCAPE

One day, Wally the whale shark went for his morning swim. Wally saw a big hole in the sand and wondered where it led. Wally raced back to his friend, Yeti Crab, and told him about the hole. Yeti Crab scurried to the hole and then was gone! Wally followed nervously. They couldn't believe their eyes. They were in an aquarium! Wally and Yeti Crab wanted to help the fish and came up with an escape plan. They led all the fish back through the hole to freedom. They had a huge party. The next day, the hole had disappeared!

Sophia Johnson (9)
Rose Hill School, Tunbridge Wells

RAPUNZEL TWIST

One day, a wicked witch adopted a baby girl; this made her happy. She called her baby girl Rapunzel and she loved her with all her heart. She took Rapunzel back to her magical mansion and gave her precious daughter the biggest room so she could dance and be free to do her art. The witch was no longer wicked, but incredibly happy when she was doing things with her daughter, Rapunzel. One of her favourite things to do was to brush Rapunzel's long hair. It took them four hours to brush it all but always with a smile.

Harriet Black (10)
Rose Hill School, Tunbridge Wells

THE GREATEST SCHOOL EVER!

This story starts in the 28th century on the border of Scotland, at a little primary school with, let's say, about fifty or so kids. Really small, right? Now, let me explain. This particular primary school wasn't what you would call normal, for a few reasons: first of all, they didn't have any lessons apart from science (only the experiments), PE (only the fun games), art and music! Secondly, they got to eat whatever they wanted at lunchtime! And finally, the main reason was that the teachers were the kids!

Isla Bysouth (11)
Rose Hill School, Tunbridge Wells

THE THREE LITTLE PIGS: THE TRUTH!

Once, in the countryside, there were three little pigs, and it was one of their birthdays. They had a massive blue cake with sparkler candles. But, uh-oh! A candle landed on the third pig's tail. "Help!" screamed the pig.

A few seconds later, the big, bad wolf came sprinting along and blew the flame out. Phew! The pigs said a big thank you to the wolf and thought he was a hero, but that was wrong. The wolf was actually trying to blow the pigs' houses down. That naughty wolf - I hate him!

Philippa Smith (8)
Rose Hill School, Tunbridge Wells

MONSTER UNDER THE BED

It all started when one day he looked under his bed, and to his horror saw a monster! He sprinted downstairs to tell his mum, but she didn't believe him. Not a single bit. They both rushed upstairs. She looked under the bed and it was not a monster. It turned out to be a human, but not any old human. It was LeBron James; a world-famous basketball player. They played basketball for roughly an hour before he figured out it was all just a dream! He ended up becoming extremely sad because LeBron James was his idol.

George Warmington (10)
Rose Hill School, Tunbridge Wells

THE CLIFFHANGER

The robber looked in his car's mirror. The policeman was gaining on him. The robber glanced at the passenger seat where the crown jewels shone in the street light. Brilliantly, he had managed to steal the jewels without anybody noticing. But now he was definitely in trouble. He took a left down a one-way street. Crowds blocked the view, so he swung down a dark, bumpy alley. The alley ended at a cliff edge. Over he went, praying. Suddenly, the car caught on a tree and dangled for a moment. A proper cliffhanger!

Max Green (9)
Rose Hill School, Tunbridge Wells

THE THREE LITTLE PIGS

Once, there were three little pigs who made houses of sticks, straw and bricks. There was a big, bad wolf who tried to blow down the houses to play 'What's the time, Mr Wolf?', but he scared the pigs. So the first pig's house was blown because the pig didn't let the wolf in, but the wolf was super nice. When the first pig's house got blown down, the pigs teamed up on the wolf and wrestled the wolf into a fire and ate the wolf up. However, more wolves came and got eaten up by the pigs!

Louie Rommer (9)
Rose Hill School, Tunbridge Wells

THE BEGGING ELF

Shadows inched closer to me. Suddenly, coldness struck my body, making me fall into the muddy leaves. I could see a bijou elf charging at me.
I got to my feet and he said, "Move out of my way!"
I did not let this elf just get past me. I picked him up by his ear but he grew until he was bigger than me, so I had to let go. I was petrified, but then I thought, *abracadabra!* He turned into his original form and I stomped as hard as possible on his toes and *boom*, he was gone!

Jude Collier (10)
Rose Hill School, Tunbridge Wells

THE TRUE STORY

Most people think of me as a villain. In this story, you'll learn the truth... Little Red was always pranking people. One day, she put hot sauce in my soup as my friends were coming around; just to embarrass me. When I told my close friend, Granny, she was furious, so we teamed up to prank Little Red. I dressed up as Granny, and she fell for it! I pretended to be all big and mean as part of the prank and she ran away scared. Everyone laughed at her, and from that day on, she never pranked anyone again.

Martha Stringer (10)
Rose Hill School, Tunbridge Wells

THE BANK ROBBERY

"The Nobel Prize goes to Gabriel Moses for donating a million pounds to a homeless charity." He looks happy as he walks up onto the stage to collect his prize.

"Breaking news! A vault has just been robbed by four masked men. One of the four has been identified as Raphael Jr, who holds a current record for the most murders."

The police threatens him, making him tell who hired him to do the job.

He says, "You wouldn't believe it, it's Gabriel Moses!"

Joseph Johnson (11)
Rose Hill School, Tunbridge Wells

THE ROOM

I walked in. A disgusting smell hit me, it was like rotten eggs and stinky socks. There was a reddish stain on the carpet and a pile of abandoned clothes. On top of a chest of drawers, a lamp with a sock hanging off it. I switched on the light; it flickered, but then it went out. I ventured forwards through the door; I could see a sink filled with brown, murky water and a toothbrush missing most of its bristles. I had to get out! I ran across the landing, back to my room. My brother was definitely messy!

Charlotte Currie (10)
Rose Hill School, Tunbridge Wells

THE STONE OF POWER

Once, there was a brave knight named Derek. He wanted to find the stone of power which would grant him unimaginable powers. He went off on his quest to find the stone. As he went into the forest, he thought what he could do with all that power. As he was looking around, he spotted a mountain, and within it, a cave. From the cave emerged a golden light which he saw coming up the mountain. He knew what he wanted to do with the stone, to rule the kingdom. Finally, he got into the cave and took the stone...

Ameer Tetley-Ahmad (9)

Rose Hill School, Tunbridge Wells

A PAPER CUT

The battle had been going on for two days, it was aliens versus humans and nobody had yet won. It was down to the last person on each side, the last remaining human was called Sean. His only weapon was an assault rifle with one shot left. The alien was called Wad, his weapon was a picture of an alien blaster. Sean shot his gun, the bullet skimmed passed Wad's ear. Then the alien threw his piece of paper at Sean and it gave him a paper cut. Sean fell on the floor... He was dead. The battle was won.

Alfie Loveday (10)
Rose Hill School, Tunbridge Wells

A WOLF'S TALE

I'm a wolf. I was great friends with an elderly lady and was due to go around to her house for tea. Unfortunately, I came down with the flu, so I went to her house to explain. She was extremely kind. She even let me sleep in her bed, whilst she went and collected flowers as her granddaughter was coming. Soon, I heard a rap at the door.
"Come in," I strained.
A girl with a red hood came in and ran out. Suddenly, a man with an axe burst in and I fled. I sprinted all the way home.

Aoife Brennan-Davey (11)
Rose Hill School, Tunbridge Wells

BROWNIELOX

I was playing in the garden alone, wishing I had a friend, when I heard a sudden crash from inside the house. I went to have a look around and I found my porridge was eaten! Despicable! To make matters worse, I found my chair was broken! Utterly despicable! I checked in my room and in my bed was a small, blonde-haired girl, sleeping. I poked her face with my paw until she stirred and snorted awake. I thought, and then it struck me! I'd found a new best friend.
"Want to go out and play?"

Maya Navarro (11)
Rose Hill School, Tunbridge Wells

BUG UNDER THE RUG

Emily lived in a small apartment in London. She was an only child, who lived with just her mum. One night, Emily was woken by strange muffling sounds. She looked down to find her slippers. However, she saw something moving under the rug! She climbed out of bed and lifted up the blue, stripy rug. There was nothing under it. She pinched herself to check she wasn't dreaming - she wasn't. When she turned around to get back into bed, there was a giant figure towering over her and she screamed...

Willow Cureton (10)
Rose Hill School, Tunbridge Wells

THE HUNGRY WOLF

Once upon a time, there was a penniless wolf who was looking for food for his family. He knocked on his neighbours' door (the pigs!), but they pretended to be out. Luckily, he found a pound on the floor and went to buy some ham. When the shop owner saw him, he chased him away. The wolf returned and tried to blow down the shop to get the food, but it was made of bricks. However, a window was open and he blew so hard that a little pig customer flew out. He and his family had bacon for tea!

Henry Whitney (9)
Rose Hill School, Tunbridge Wells

JUST KEEP RUNNING

I walked down the corridor of the mall. As a security guard, I knew that even though nobody was there, I still had to patrol. I looked at my watch, 3am it said. Behind me, an almighty bang made me turn around to what may be my last look at the mall. There was a creature, I immediately ran for my life. I knew the mall very well but couldn't find an exit. Suddenly, I saw an exit sign. Even though I had not seen this exit before, I went through the door and found myself in my bedroom...

Alfred Churcher (9)
Rose Hill School, Tunbridge Wells

THE MONSTER IN THE PARK

The monster was finally dead. It had taken days of work to trap and kill the monster. I was relieved that all of humanity was saved forever. The lake was finally finished. After the intense trap that took a whole day to set up, the tourist attraction was now open. Soon after that, I was walking down the path when I suddenly heard a scream. I was worried, so I ran over as fast as possible to see the monster roaring furiously. The SWAT team arrived. At that moment, all turned to black...

Caelan Cravero (10)
Rose Hill School, Tunbridge Wells

ANDY THE AMAZING ANT!

Being an ant is hard. You can easily get squashed if you're not careful. But an ant named Andy was walking along a busy street in London when an extremely tall man was running and squashed him! Andy knew that one day this would happen but then he felt himself growing and growing and he just kept on growing until he was as tall as a giraffe! After a while, Andy started getting used to his new body and to make use of it, he stopped all crimes and became the protector of the world!

Victoria Hajian (9)
Rose Hill School, Tunbridge Wells

ANNA AND THE FLYING MANSION

Once upon a time, there was a girl called Anna. She was playing football one day when there was an alien abduction. Anna and her friends were petrified. They found themselves at a flying mansion. Then Anna found a hallway. It was very intimidating. It was like a prison. Anna did so much work to escape by finding three keys. A cat led her to a mirror. Then the alien used one of his powers. The mirror broke and there was a portal. Anna jumped through, screaming for help as she fell...

Thomas Smart (10)
Rose Hill School, Tunbridge Wells

JUST A NORMAL DAY AT SCHOOL?

One morning, the children went to school and did their normal daily things, but at lunch, something strange happened... The teachers all went into different rooms and... *bam!* The food came alive and the children knew they were in trouble... The broccoli took one look at Charlie's scrumptious head and chomped down! Mazy stared the tomato in the eye. It leapt into Mazy's mouth and burst open, with hot sauce scorching Mazy's mouth. Revenge was sweet!

Camilla Wade (9)
Rose Hill School, Tunbridge Wells

THE SCHOOL MINOTAUR

One day, I was in Saint John's School, learning English, when I saw a mysterious pencil. Suddenly, a minotaur came out of it. I was frightened. I sprinted down the corridor. I ran. I hid, but I couldn't escape. It was basically impossible. Just when I was just about to give up, I saw a secret door. But of course, it was on the other side of the school. I pelted myself over to the door. The minotaur was right behind me so I went in. Where would it lead me?

Joseph Clayton (9)
Rose Hill School, Tunbridge Wells

THE MYSTERIOUS METEORITE

I was immersed in my book; I looked up, seeing a flash. The car felt intensely hot. I was perplexed. Suddenly, something smashed into me. I was in excruciating pain and everything went black. Days or months later, I awoke in a hospital bed with a serious-looking man sitting next to me. It was almost as if he had been waiting there the whole time. He asked me about the meteorite. I was clueless as to what he was talking about. A meteorite hit my car?

Max Bailey (10)
Rose Hill School, Tunbridge Wells

JACK AND THE BROKEN BEANSTALK

While Jack was climbing down the beanstalk for the third time, he felt a wobble. Bravely, he carried on going. When he had almost reached the bottom, the beanstalk started shaking and swaying. From his enormous castle, the giant heard the commotion and came outside to check. "What's happening?"

"Help!" cried Jack, holding on for dear life.

"Here, grab my hand!" said the giant.

Jack took the giant's hand and climbed back up.

"Now," said the giant, "do you have any idea who stole my golden goose?" From inside Jack's satchel came a clucking noise.

"Nope," he smiled.

Sunho Kim (10)
St Helen's Primary School, Swansea

RAVENOUS RED RIDING HOOD

Little Red Riding Hood was heading to her grandmother's house. On her way, she met the Big Bad Wolf.

"Come with me to my grandmother's house," said Red.

"It would be my pleasure," grinned the wolf, thinking he would eat both Red and her grandmother for his tea.

When they arrived, Red trapped the wolf, and to his horror, Red and her grandmother transformed into hideous werewolves. The wolf cried in fear.

"Well done, Red," said Grandmother, "you've brought us dinner."

Red smiled and licked her lips.

"We can share," she said, and they pounced on the wolf!

Mohi Khan (11)
St Helen's Primary School, Swansea

THE THREE CANNIBAL PIGS

After a long day of work, the Three Little Pigs found their father talking to his best friend, the Wolf, on the doorstep. Daddy Pig and the Wolf chatted and laughed, talking all about the dinner they'd eaten. This made the Three Little Pigs very hungry.

"We've been working all day," they said, "is our dinner ready?"

"I'm sorry," said Daddy Pig, "I invited Mr Wolf around for dinner and we ate all the food."

The Three Little Pigs were furious and they decided to eat their father for their dinner.

"Bacon sandwiches for tea!" shouted one of the pigs.

Tobias Baldwin (10)
St Helen's Primary School, Swansea

GOLDILOCKS THE ASSASSIN

As the bears were leaving their home, Goldilocks crept in through an open window. Bears were very predictable. She sneaked around the home, eating their porridge for breakfast, sat on their favourite chairs, and even bounced on their beds. Goldilocks carried a scroll with her, full of instructions. Her boss, the leader of the assassin's gang, had told her not to return empty-handed.

"Come home with three bears' heads, or don't come back at all."

She waited, and when the bears returned, she did not expect them to be as powerful as they were. Goldilocks wouldn't survive this fight...

Mohammath Faris (11)

St Helen's Primary School, Swansea

THE ETERNAL SLEEP

Long ago, Princess Aurora pricked her finger on the spindle of a spinning wheel and fell into eternal sleep. It was Prince Phillip's job to bestow upon the princess true love's kiss. News of the sleeping princess travelled to the far kingdoms. Even Prince Charming heard the news. He made it his mission to save the sleeping beauty. He spent days and nights travelling to reach his destination, only to be confronted by a powerful, evil enchantress. She killed Prince Charming in cold blood and Aurora slumbered for all eternity. No other prince was brave enough to dare save her...

Ayesha Rahman (11)
St Helen's Primary School, Swansea

CINDERELLA'S MISTAKE

One autumn night, Prince Charming threw a ball for all the women in his kingdom. From far and wide, women came to the ball in their most elegant dresses. Nobody more than Cinderella wanted to attend. With the help of the magical Fairy Godmother, Cinderella was able to go, but under one condition. Cinderella must be home before midnight! Whilst there, the clock ticked and ticked, but Cinderella paid no notice. The clock struck midnight, and just as the prince leaned in for a kiss, the magic wore off. Before his eyes, Cinderella transformed into a dirty, smelly, ashy housemaid.

Sarai Cox (10)
St Helen's Primary School, Swansea

RAPUNZEL'S CHOICE

One dark, gloomy night an old Sorceress called Gargarella crept into the Royal Castle. She stole the baby Prince Russell from his crib and made off with him into the night. Years passed and Russell grew up thinking Gargarella was his mother. He had no idea that Gargarella had stolen him to use the power of his golden curls. His golden hair gave Gargarella the power to turn anything she wanted to gold. When Russell found out his mother's true intentions, he touched his mother's hand and, before his eyes, Gargarella turned to solid gold.

Alannah-Jo Owen (10)
St Helen's Primary School, Swansea

RAPUNZEL'S REVENGE

Long ago, the legend of Rapunzel's magical, golden hair was well-known across the land. From all over, thieves and bandits came to her tower to try and claim the magic hair as their own. One day, a handsome prince arrived and persuaded her to let down her hair. He climbed up the long strands, but when he reached her room, he snatched up a pair of scissors, cutting her hair off in one snip. Just then, Rapunzel's mother arrived home and forced the prince to drink a magic potion. In an instant, he was transformed into a slimy, green frog.

Dawud Hussain (10)

St Helen's Primary School, Swansea

THE BROKEN EARTH

One million years ago, when brutal gladiators and Romans fought outside of the ancient ruins, the leaders of both sides' swords touched, then... *boom!* The swords came together, making an amazing sword. It sliced down and split the world in half. Sinking down into the Earth, never to be seen again. 79,000 years later, someone for the first time ever crossed the crack in the Earth; he started, but then he fell. Landing straight by the sword. Wishing he had backup, he looked down... "*No!*"

He pulled the sword up, out of Earth. *Boom!* The planet was back to normal.

Roman Jenkins (10)

Tushingham-With-Grindley CE Primary School, Tushingham

JACK

Jack lived with his mum. He traded his cow for magical beans. His mum got mad; she threw them out the window! Jack climbed the beanstalk that grew, stole a golden-egg-laying chicken and a golden harp who sang, waking the giant up! The chase was on! He ran through the large castle as fast as he possibly could.

"Fee-fi-fo-fum, I can't wait to have you in my tum!" the giant roared.

Jack reached the big, green beanstalk... *Crunch!* The giant ate Jack! He plunged into the dark abyss of the giant's stomach. That was the last time anyone saw Jack.

Harry Buxton (10)

Tushingham-With-Grindley CE Primary School, Tushingham

THE MYSTERIOUS HOUSE NEXT DOOR

A group of friends plucked up the courage to go and explore inside the feared house down the street. The oak door creaked open. The leader of the group, Lucas, took a step inside. Suddenly, he vanished. His scream echoed, a worried look spread across the boys' faces.

"Wake up, Lucas, it's time for school, you're going to be late."

Startled, Lucas sat up. As he looked out the window, to his surprise, a new house had appeared. He recognised it.

"Oh no, it can't be the same one from my dream, can it? I need to warn them!"

Georgia Paul (11)
Tushingham-With-Grindley CE Primary School, Tushingham

PERSEUS AND MEDUSA

Once, there was a powerful monster called Medusa who turned enemies to stone. Perseus, a strong demigod, was ordered to hunt down Medusa with a celestial bronze sword. He travelled many miles to find the palace of Medusa; upon arrival at the palace, he was greeted by a 150m stone tower. The stone was weird, like there were people in its concrete: Medusa's enemies... Perseus would have to be careful. He was soon inside the castle and found himself in the same room as Medusa, face-to-face with her, and was turned to stone; destined to spend eternity in the wall...

Holly Probin (11)
Tushingham-With-Grindley CE Primary School, Tushingham

THE DISAPPEARANCE OF SARAH KAY

The night that Sarah Kay went missing, there were numerous reports of an old China doll with a sharp knife clutched in its palm, sitting at the edge of her windowsill. Sarah was afraid of dolls so it was unusual for the family to own one. That night, the neighbour witnessed a lullaby being sung by a blurry figure sitting on Sarah's wooden rocking chair. In the morning, the parents were found dead next to their child's room, but their child was undiscovered. The doll was found sitting on Sarah's bed, blood on its ice-cold hands and around its mouth...

Emmy Shaw (11)
Tushingham-With-Grindley CE Primary School, Tushingham

THE BRANDERSHAUN TERROR

Billy was a normal type of person in an average town. But one day, that all changed when a strange object was stolen from the museum. Still, people lived life normally like nothing happened. But it started to get *bad*, actual people started to go missing, like the nice old lady that ran the store. So the council decided that we, every night, must lock our door. Billy woke up in the middle of the night, hearing noises by the door. He grabbed his new bat. The door opened. There was mechanical chomping and grappling claws with glowing red eyes...

Freddie Parton (10)
Tushingham-With-Grindley CE Primary School, Tushingham

THE TALKING CAKE

One chilly night, a young girl, Martha, was having an amazing sleep when all of a sudden, she was rudely woken by a strange, loud noise. Martha got out of her snuggly bed to see what was going on; as she reached the bottom of the stairs, the noise started again, but this time it was much quieter. It was coming from the kitchen, it looked like the cake had moved. Martha put it back where it first was; until it started to speak.

"Hello, my name is Cake," it exclaimed while smiling.

Martha started to scream and ran upstairs...

Caoimhe Cronin (10)
Tushingham-With-Grindley CE Primary School, Tushingham

NANCY FAIRY AND STEVE THE DOG

The house up the street had been haunted for years, no one ever had the courage to go near it. The tale of the house was the old Kreel house was massive. It held four people inside. Quickly, the house became haunted. Their peace was very quickly ruined... One evening, the Kreel family sat down for tea.

The youngest shouted, "Nancy Fairy and Steve the Dog, save us from our death!"

There was a poof. Nancy Fairy and Steve the Dog showed up and a massive wave flew over the house and everything went back to normal.

Lola Beckett (10)

Tushingham-With-Grindley CE Primary School, Tushingham

A SPOOKY CIRCUS

Before time, a circus of darkness was created. No one could destroy it. It was implanted on Earth's dome forever. One day, there was a girl who went to the circus and was never seen again. From then on, people stopped going to the circus. But little did they know, the millions of people who went to the circus thinking the show was going to be the best day of their life instead found their souls stuck in the underground, haunting the life out of the workers and warning off any visitors who dared to make the same mistake...

Frances Hearn (9)

Tushingham-With-Grindley CE Primary School, Tushingham

MUSHROOM FOREST

Hello, my name's Belle! It's a cold winter day and I'll tell you all about my mushroom forest! I love hanging out in my mushroom home with all my forest friends. Most of the time, I hang out with the friendly foxes because they have a whale of a time. I hang all of my belongings on all of the branches. Most of the time, I have to save the animals because they're so clumsy! Like yesterday, Mr Blackbird was terribly stuck; he was clawed to the branch, so I had to save him. I did, and that was that!

Elsie Wilkinson (9)
Tushingham-With-Grindley CE Primary School, Tushingham

JUB

Jub had brown eyes, black hair and long arms. After a long, busy night, Jub climbed up her big old oak tree to get to her warm, cosy, big hole. She read her old and favourite book about witches, and then she washed her clothes and hung them up on her washing line. After that, she had some food, but while she was eating, the birds were humming sleepy tunes. She slept well all night, dreaming of witches. The next day, she was upset because there was a witch in the forest; had it come from her magical dream?

Erica Clark (9)

Tushingham-With-Grindley CE Primary School, Tushingham

THE STRAY KITTEN

One chilly day, William was skipping around his local park. All of a sudden, he heard a noise coming from the bin. William went to investigate, but when he looked inside, there was a cute little ginger stray kitten. It was a girl and William picked her up. He decided to take her back to give her some food and a clean. He looked in his fridge to see if he had any spare milk and he had around 150ml, so he put it in a bowl so she could have a drink as she hadn't drank in a while.

Mckenzie Walker (11)

Tushingham-With-Grindley CE Primary School, Tushingham

JUB AND THE HAPPY ENDINGS

Jub was a little girl who lived in a hole in a tree and hated the bad endings of books. So every day, she had a job to get all the bad endings and climb up a tree to tip out them. Sadly, most mornings they blew back and she had a horrible day. She went for a walk and came home and read the book she was reading about flowers. Strangely, footsteps started coming closer and closer, she was very worried. It was a wolf, so she turned it into a big lump of cream and was very happy.

Alfie Dratwinski (10)
Tushingham-With-Grindley CE Primary School, Tushingham

THE GOOD SOLDIER

There was a man-eating horse that was evil, he always ate the people that he could see. The people were scared of him, of course they were. The thing was, he didn't do it all the time, he did it when he was angry. His best food was the pigs next door. Then, one day, the people had a plan to kill the horseman. The next day he came out, the people went to action. They set up a trapdoor and he fell down. The people ate him.

Harvey Williamson (9)
Tushingham-With-Grindley CE Primary School, Tushingham

JOSH'S DAY

Today, Josh was in Tushingham and there were people missing, so Josh was super worried about the mighty monster. One day, Josh got grabbed and went to a school of good or evil. Luckily, Josh went to... good! So he was a prince, but if he went to evil, he would have been a bully. Sadly, his friend went to evil school so he became a bully and he saw him. Josh was happy and sad that his only friend had become evil.

Josh Wilkinson (10)
Tushingham-With-Grindley CE Primary School, Tushingham

THE KNIGHT IN BLACK

The knight in black, the legendary hero and god slayer. They killed gods who disobeyed the warnings of those that obeyed, but one day they vanished without a trace. Twenty years later, there was a boy named Adam. Adam wasn't like other kids, he was the son of the black knight...

Dayton Meredith (10)

Tushingham-With-Grindley CE Primary School, Tushingham